"Samantha Hunt's every sentence electrifies. Her book contains everything that I want in a novel. If I could long-distance mesmerize you, dear reader, into picking up this book and buying it and reading it at once, believe me: I would."   —Kelly Link

"[*Mr. Splitfoot*] will haunt me . . . Hypnotic and glowing."
          —Gregory Maguire, *The New York Times Book Review*

"The way I feel about Samantha Hunt's *Mr. Splitfoot* is how one of its characters describes meeting his wife: 'We fell in love in a bloody way, thorns and hooks.' "
          —Daniel Johnson, *The Paris Review* (Staff Pick)

"The historical and the fantastical entwine like snakes . . . There's a rare pleasure in this blend of romance and phantoms."   —Ron Charles, *The Washington Post*

"Gripping . . . 'History holds up one side of our lives and fiction the other,' one character tells Cora, and the novel's pleasures lie in the intersections between the two."
                                        —*The New Yorker*

"At once an intriguing mystery with clues, suspense, enigmas galore, and an exhilarating, witty, poignant paean to

the unexplainable, the unsolvable, the irreducibly mysterious."   —Priscilla Gilman, *The Boston Globe*

"A wild ride. If you're all about magical realists like Kelly
Link, this is one title you'll need to pick up, because Samantha Hunt's third novel takes the banal and rockets it
into the fantastic (and the fantastically wonderful)."

—*Bustle*

"A riveting, linguistically playful tale about demons (real
or imagined), loss, magic and motherhood."

—Zoë Apostolides, *Financial Times*

"An American Gothic fever dream . . . Hunt's packed prose
writhes with hallucinatory detail. At her best, she lurches
from lyricism to cynicism in short, declarative sentences."

—Amy Gentry, *Chicago Tribune*

"Hunt maintains a dark and disturbing atmosphere
throughout this intriguing, well-drawn gothic."

—Connie Ogle, *The Miami Herald*

"Ethereal . . . This spellbinder is storytelling at its best."

—*Publishers Weekly* (starred review)

"A truly fantastic novel in which the blurring of natural
and supernatural creates a stirring, visceral conclusion."

—*Kirkus Reviews* (starred review)

"Samantha Hunt's new book is a revelation. It's emotion-
ally precise, brilliantly imagined and flat-out spooky. A

gothic novel that somehow manages to feel thrillingly contemporary and wholly original." —Jenny Offill

"I'm speechless. *Mr. Splitfoot* is so inventive, so *new*; I haven't read anything like it in years . . . It's a thrilling page-turner. I couldn't stop reading it." —Gary Shteyngart

"*Mr. Splitfoot* is lyrical, echoing, deeply strange, with a quality of sustained hallucination. It is the best book on communicating with the dead since William Lindsay Gresham's *Nightmare Alley*, but it swaps out that novel's cynicism for a more life-affirming sense of uncertainty."

—Luc Sante

"Absolutely thrilling . . . Hunt gives us plenty of humor amid the horror and awe—and then turns on the lights and shows us what was looming above us the whole time. I can't stop thinking about it." —Sarah Manguso

The Invention of Everything Else

Winner, Bard Fiction Prize

Finalist for the Orange Prize

Long-listed for the IMPAC Dublin Literary Award, 2010

A *Washington Post* Best Book of 2008

"Dazzling." —Elissa Schappel, *Vanity Fair*

"A sophisticated pastiche of science fiction, fantasy, melodrama, and historical anecdote . . . It all adds up to a precocious math of human marvel." —*Elle*

"Glorious . . . Daring and delicious, perfectly calibrated, fresh but not raw, original but neither off-putting nor disconcertingly strange."   —Beth Kephart, *Chicago Tribune*

The Seas
National Book Foundation's 5 Under 35 Award

"One of the most distinctive and unforgettable voices I've read in years. This book will linger . . . in your head for a good long time."   —Dave Eggers

THE
DARK
DARK

THE
DARK
DARK

STORIES

SAMANTHA HUNT

corsair

CORSAIR

First published in the US in 2017 by Farrar, Straus and Giroux
First published in Great Britain in 2018 by Corsair

1 3 5 7 9 10 8 6 4 2

Copyright © 2017 by Samantha Hunt

The moral right of the author has been asserted.

A CIP catalogue record for this book
is available from the British Library.

ISBN: 978-1-4721-5425-5

Designed by Jonathan D. Lippincott
Printed and bound in Great Britain by
CPI Group (UK) Ltd., Croydon, CR0 4YY

Papers used by Corsair are from well-managed forests
and other responsible sources.

Corsair
An imprint of
Little, Brown Book Group
Carmelite House
50 Victoria Embankment
London EC4Y 0DZ

An Hachette UK Company
www.hachette.co.uk

www.littlebrown.co.uk

For Norma Stallings Nolan Santangelo,
the bright bright

Then she raised the hoe above her head.

—Eudora Welty

CONTENTS

THE

DARK
DARK

THE STORY OF

In a coffee shop on Dead Elm Street, Norma arranges
chicken bones on her plate, making an arrow that points to
her stomach, where the chicken now resides. She once saw
a picture of a hen in a science book. The hen had been split
open down the breast, unzipped like a parka. Inside was
a chain of eggs, rubbery as tapioca, small getting smaller
until they almost disappeared. Nothing like the basket of
fried chicken Norma has just finished eating, but sickening
all the same.

The waitress says, "If it's all the same to you I'll—"

"It's never all the same." Norma's thinking of the eggs.
"It changes a tiny bit every time."

But the waitress keeps talking. "—just close out your
check, 'cause we're switching shifts."

Outside, cars slow to the stop sign. Dead Elm Street
is not a dead-end street, but Norma imagines a remedy, a
couple of concrete barriers that could cut Dead Elm in half,

leaving behind North Dead Elm and South Dead Elm, two streets instead of one. Inconvenient for getting across town, but satisfying: Dead Elm the dead end. Procreation by division, just like the amoebae.

"Wait. Do you have any walnuts?" Norma asks.

"Walnuts?"

"Walnuts."

"No. No walnuts, no pecans, no filberts. No nuts. Walnuts?" the waitress asks again.

"They get you pregnant."

"Walnuts get you pregnant?"

"I read it on the Internet."

The waitress curls her mouth into a half-smile like she's saying, *I doubt it.* She's a pretty waitress but all of her good looks didn't make her a genius, so Norma wonders what the heck the waitress knows about the health benefits of walnuts.

Norma eats lunch here every day since she lost her job. She and the waitress often talk. They are used to each other the way people are used to their TV sets, a hum that keeps them warm even if they aren't listening to the broadcast.

Norma slides out of the booth.

The stalls in the ladies' room are made of aluminum. Norma rests her head against this coolness while she pees. In the stall wall she can see a distorted reflection of herself. The dark chestnut hair dye she tried last week makes every minor bump and blemish on her pale face bright red, raw as a goth girl. The hairs on her cheeks seem unnaturally white and furry next to her nearly black hair. While she picks at her skin she feels something familiar—a peeling, a pain. In the toilet a streamer of blood sinks to the bottom of the bowl, a dark, dead fish.

Yesterday Norma asked the waitress how long it took her to get pregnant and the waitress said, "I don't know. Fifteen minutes?"

"No. I mean, how many times did you have to try?"

And she said, "Try? What do you mean, honey?"

The waitress has three kids. She doesn't seem to like any of them.

Norma's been trying to get pregnant for over two years, and each time she gets her period a small bit of strength leaks out of her. Iron and blood. Each month she thinks maybe it worked this time. She'll walk very carefully up stairs and avoid lifting anything heavy. Just in case. But then, every month her period comes, a cellar door slamming shut. Something is not working and Norma does not want to go to the doctor to find out what. She doesn't want medical confirmation saying she'll never be able to have children. She'd rather keep some hope intact. But hope is very hard to do.

Norma's shoulders have begun to slump. Her eyes often shift between what she is looking at and the ground. It's cold comfort, but Norma imagines the deaths these non-babies would have had to die had they ever been born: car crashes, heart disease, cerebral hemorrhage. At least she has spared her non-babies all that dying.

And no one *needs* a baby. The survival of the species is not at risk, so Norma says nothing about all this wanting even when Ted, her own husband, acts like an asshole.

"I'm ovulating," Norma will tell him while staring at the bedroom carpet, humiliated. And Ted groans from a place so low in his belly, a place where he stores the worst pains, as if to say any chore would be preferable, taking out the garbage, vacuuming the basement, regrouting the tub. *Please*. Norma stands on the sides of her feet to feel the ache all the way down in her skeleton.

In the bathroom stall, she zips her pants up, grabs her stomach, shaking it a little, poking her belly. "Hey," she says in the empty bathroom. "Wake up, ovaries."

There's a message, graffiti on the wall. GIVE ME A CALL. 1-800-FUCKIN'A. She dials the number on her cell phone.

"Hello?"

"Hi. 1-800-FUCKIN'A?"

"No. Sorry. We're 1-800-DUBL-INC. Doubles Incorporated, providing goods and services for the Procreation by Division Industries."

"Procreation by division?"

"Yeah. You know. Like the amoebae."

Norma hangs up so quickly it may be possible that the phone call never even happened.

On the way home Norma walks past a number of construction sites and some old farms where the grass grows as high as her waist. Strip malls, hills, grasshoppers, people, they all multiply. Norma bites her nails and spits the bits into the rounded, ripe fields. She leaves a trail of her DNA.

A rustling speeds up behind her like an enormous snake. Norma turns. A woman is pedaling quite furiously on a tiny BMX bike with fluorescent green tires, looking like some half-mad delivery person. Her chin is stuck out in front of her like an ape. Her face is sharp. The blades of her cheekbones have been accentuated by two brutish swaths of rouge. The woman wears her dark hair feathered back with a bandana rolled and tied across her forehead as if fashions had not changed since 1981. She looks tough, dirty, terrified. Perhaps even a little bit retarded. Her eyes are watery and distracted as an addict's.

Though they are the only two people on the road, the woman stares straight ahead. She clenches her lips around a cigarette while she pedals, one hand on the handlebars. She doesn't blink. She glides past Norma and is gone.

Creepy, but creepy like a humongous pile of insects crawling all over one another, a pile of insects Norma would want to stare at or poke with a long stick.

A few summers back Norma and Ted moved into a development called Rancho de Caza. It was what they could afford and Ted promised they wouldn't spend their whole lives living in a development. At the time, Rancho de Caza was not a gated community. Norma had insisted on that. But then there was a spate of burglaries, and after a thirty-eight-year-old mother from Lilac Lane was lashed to a kitchen chair with duct tape and thrown into her swimming pool, the board of Rancho de Caza changed their minds. Even though the woman lived. Now when Norma walks home she must stand in front of the guardhouse, wave to the man inside, and wait while he swings open two white wrought-iron gates big enough for an eighteen-wheeler. The gates make

Norma feel like a mouse entering a giant's city. They close behind her. She scurries down Day Lily Street before taking a left on Daffodil.

Rancho de Caza has certain rules, bylaws. Grass must be cut. No lawn ornaments bigger than one and one-half feet. No unapproved swing sets. No compost piles. Two trees maximum per yard. Norma and Ted got lucky. They have a nice tall sycamore that shades the Mediterranean roof tiles. All the houses in Rancho de Caza have Mediterranean roof tiles. The sycamore's leaves are larger than Ted's hand, so large a neighbor once complained that Ted and Norma should pay for his Guatemalan lawn guy because one of the development's laws is: leaves must be raked, bagged, and thrown away once a week from October 1 to November 31. "They're not my leaves," the neighbor said. Norma and Ted stared blankly over the low fence that divided the properties, hoping if they ignored the matter it would go away.

Caza. What a bunch of idiots.

It's not really the same old story: bored couple in suburbia. Norma loves Ted. He is very kind. He looks a bit like a news anchor, or maybe a local TV weatherman, a tennis pro. Handsome first, then well-groomed, then smart.

When Ted and Norma first met he was still living at home with his parents, growing hydroponic marijuana in the family basement. He was twenty-six at the time and made a living driving the local library's bookmobile to the rougher parts of the city and out to the old folks' home. Sometimes Norma would ride in the van with him. They'd get high in the bookmobile, flip through the children's books together, and make out. Norma loved to watch Ted as he helped little redneck girls or senile old men pick out something good to read in the van where she and Ted had just been kissing. It all seemed so generous. People always left the van surprised. "You mean, I can just take this book?" And Ted would nod yes, yes, you can.

But then Ted turned twenty-seven, and two days after his birthday his father asked to have a word with Ted and his mother. Ted's father confessed that he had another family, a whole other family, another wife, another house, and another kid, a girl, only she wasn't a girl anymore, she was a woman. All these years, all those sales calls and business trips were lies. Even the two Christmases he'd claimed to be caught in Chicago snowstorms. He was lying. He was a few towns away at his other family's house. Ted's father said he was sorry. He said he wasn't quite sure how things had gotten so out of control. Ted's father said that the new sister was anxious to meet her sibling. Ted didn't believe that for an instant. His father said he felt great. He'd been wanting to tell them for so long. He was relieved that the telling was over. Ted's mother said Ted's father was lower than the lowest species of worm and then threw him out of the house. "And if you ever think about coming back or even calling, don't," she said. "I'll buy a gun and if I can't get a gun I'll just use a piece of broken glass to gouge your eyes out while you sleep."

Ted woke up the following morning, went to the basement, and ripped up every single stalk of marijuana he had growing there. He took the plants out back to the leaf pile and set the whole thing on fire. Ted bought his first suit and filled out three applications for entry-level management positions, one at a wholesale imported food distributor, one at a textile company, and one at a home supply warehouse. He didn't get any of the jobs, but the next week he went and filled out three more applications. Then he asked Norma to marry him, and Norma, also shaken by the news that someone's entire life can be a lie, said yes. She loved Ted.

Last night Norma and Ted had chicken breasts, broccoli, and couscous for dinner. Later, when the development went quiet, Ted stepped outside. Norma didn't know what he was doing out there—surveying the property for wild beasts or burglars—but when he came back he smelled like fresh air. Ted and Norma went to bed and held each other underneath the covers.

Home from the diner, she checks the messages. "Hi, Norm, are you there? Are you there? I guess you're not there." Outside, an airplane passes overhead, making a shadow on her back lawn. She watches it go and the house is quiet again.

Earlier she'd been surfing the Web, looking at a TTC, Trying to Conceive, chat room.

> **baby@43**: thanks to clomid I tried to shove DH down the stairs yesterday.
> **sterile ms.**: just found out health insurance won't pay for my two $15,000 IVFs that didn't work
> **wannabb**: implantation bleeding? anyone?

baby@43: implantation bleeding is a myth spread
by women who have no trouble conceiving.
there's no such thing, wannabb. that's yer period

Women are mean to each other in the TTC chat
rooms. Even Norma can get mean. She'll type in, *Good
luck* to someone, but she doesn't mean it plainly. She means
it more like *Fat chance. You're too old. Much older than me.
You're never going to have a baby.*

She looks past her computer, out into the backyard.
There is something in the tree. Something large and dark.
It is a mass like cancer or a squirrel's nest. She lets her eyes
focus. And there it is, and she couldn't be more surprised.
It's a beautiful hawk, a tremendous, beautiful, speckle-
breasted hawk come to visit Rancho de Caza. In all the
years that Norma has lived in this development she has
seen goldfinches, blue jays, cardinals even, pigeons, sparrows,
swallows, starlings, crows, grosbeaks, and wrens, but she has
never seen a bird of prey. It's preening its breast on a high
branch. Norma can make out its bright yellow talons and
beak, its long tail of secure feathers.

"What are you doing here?" Then, as certainly as if the
hawk had answered her itself, she knows. "You're here to
tell me that I'm going to have a baby, aren't you?" Norma
says it out loud to confirm the bird's meaning. She feels all
the weight in her arms, all the gloom of getting her period
disappear. "Thank you." She's sure of the sign, so she picks
up the cordless phone to make it real.

"Ted Jonsen, please.

"Hi.

"You won't believe it.

"No. There's a hawk in the backyard.

"I know.

"Yeah, I'm sure. It's huge.

"It's huge.

"Nothing.

"Damica? They're coming this weekend.

"I think the hawk is a good—

"What?

"Umm, I think Saturday.

"Maybe some cranberry juice.

"Okay.

"Okay. See you soon.

"Yup. Bye."

Norma hangs up and her heart snags. The sign seems less certain now. The bird is gone, and Norma wishes she'd done things differently. Take a bit of good news and Norma will always spread it out thin over the telephone lines, until all she has left is a small smudge, a quickly fading memory of the color yellow and the white-speckled feathers.

There's a few chat strings streaming in front of her: HSGs, D&Cs, OPKs, and BBTs. There is also a box you can click to send someone who is TTC some Baby Dust. It's a virtual gift that arrives over e-mail. Norma already sent herself some a couple of months ago. Storks, smiley faces, pink and blue bits of electronic confetti. It didn't work. Do cancer websites have asinine toys like that? Chemo dust to sprinkle for a cure?

She looks away from her computer again and there in the backyard is a BMX bicycle with fluorescent-green tires, one wheel spinning slowly in the breeze. Norma steps out the back slider barefoot, her toes in the warm grass. No one's there. She looks up through the branches of the syca-more tree. Nothing. Norma rights her neck.

The woman with the addict eyes stares at Norma. She's no more than two narrow feet away. She looks like she's hungry.

"You scared me." Norma keeps her voice calm and friendly the way one might with a cruel dog.

Norma sees now that the woman is filthy. Tiny capillary lines of sweaty grit swoop across her neck like a tidal shore. Her fingernails are rimmed with dirt as if she crawled out of a grave. There's a large dark birthmark on the woman's collarbone. It could be the mother ship, the epicenter of all this dirt. The woman is missing a side tooth, a dark hole that sucks in all of Norma's attention.

There is a power to her filth that keeps Norma from screaming or calling the cops. There's power in the woman's lacy black tank top, in her cutoff corduroys and oversized camouflage coat.

"You scared me," Norma repeats herself. The woman is breathing heavily. "Can I help you with something?"

"What's your name again?" the woman asks, as if Norma had already volunteered this information.

Hypnotized by the missing tooth, Norma answers. "Norma. What's yours?"

"Huh. Norma."

"Yes. What's your name?"

"Norma. Are you deaf?"

"That's my name."

"Well. It's my name also."

The woman cracks her knuckles. She kicks at something underfoot. A starling titters from a tree and Norma wonders why the camo coat. Norma doesn't believe her. "I've never met another Norma in my life."

"I'm an old friend of Ted's. Can I get something to drink?" Dirty Norma asks. "I've been riding my bike."

Norma considers offering her the garden hose until she remembers her manners. "Yes, of course," Norma says. "A glass of water."

"Got any soda?" She follows Norma inside the sliding back door.

"A soda."

"Yeah."

"Okay. All right," Norma says. "A soda." They file into the kitchen. Norma doesn't keep soda in the fridge but she's got a can in the pantry. "You live around here?" Norma wonders about the guard, how she got past.

"No. You like it?"

"There's a lot of rules. We're not going to stay here forever."

"What rules?"

"You're not allowed to have more than two trees in your yard."

"That's the stupidest thing I've ever heard."

"I know."

"So then why do you do it?" Dirty Norma asks. "Why don't you just start planting lots of trees? What are they going to do? Come dig them up? Take away your trees?"

Norma has been standing in the pantry door, looking

into the darkness for a can of soda. She finds one and closes the door. She crosses the kitchen and hands her the can and a glass of ice. Dirty Norma's bare toes are filthy in their flip-flops. They hold the remnants of some dark purple nail polish. Norma stares at these toes against the beige and cream linoleum until she hears the pop of the can. There is the hiss of the bubbles. There are the gulping breaths of air as Dirty Norma swallows the entire soda without ever putting it on ice. She hands Norma the can, the cold, unused glass. Dirty Norma belches and Norma can smell the corn syrup on her breath.

"Why don't I give Ted a call?"

"Go right ahead."

So Norma does, taking the cordless into the dining room, out of earshot.

"Hi. So, there's a friend of yours here.

"Uhh, Norma.

"Yeah weird, right?"

Norma lowers her voice to a dead whisper. "How do you know her?

"But.

"I see.

"Fine, tell me later."

When she hangs up, Dirty Norma is no longer standing in the kitchen. Norma hears the television in the living room. Dirty Norma has made herself at home. She's watching the end of a talk show. The topic is BULLIES. Norma stands behind her, staring at the woman's head. Her hair is matted with grease. Dirty Norma turns. "Hope you don't mind I turned on the tube."

"Make yourself at home," Norma says. "Ted'll be here soon."

Dirty Norma points her index finger at Norma, a gun, a finger parting the hedge. *You're lonely. Just like me.* "So, you want to have a baby," she says. Dirty Norma jerks her chin toward the computer screen. The monitor's been shaken awake, someone's hand on the mouse.

And Norma nods her head yes. This woman does not seem to be the sort who might say, *Oh, I just know it's going to work out for you soon!* So Norma decides to tell her about it. She's trying to formulate words that explain what her life without a baby feels like, but none of the words are right. *It hurts. It's unjust.* That sounds dumb. *Teenagers are locking their newborns in broom closets.* Also dumb. *Infertility is death doled out in tiny, monthly doses.* The clock on the microwave flashes 12:11, as if it's counting down.

"That's kind of like the trouble I've got," Dirty Norma says.

And Norma stops wondering what this woman is doing here. The universe works in mysterious ways. First the hawk, then the other Norma. Norma's face opens wide, her arms, her heart. "You can't get pregnant either? Oh, Norma. Oh. It sucks, right? It's awful. And think of all those years you tried to *not* have a baby, right? And the—"

"No." Dirty Norma smiles slightly. Screech goes the world. "I need to get unpregnant."

"Unpregnant." Norma's dry lips stick together.

"Yeah. I thought Ted could help me."

"Ted?"

"Yeah."

"How?"

"I need some money."

"Oh."

"Ted's my brother."

The air has fled Norma's lungs. Even this meth-head disaster of a human being can get pregnant. There is frozen, hardened steel in Norma's veins. Unwanted cells divide and multiply in Dirty Norma's belly. Norma backs away, fearing a fog of violence. Norma imagines blood, clawing the sides of her thighs as she leaves. "There's more soda if you want."

Ted ducks his head back into his car, reaching across the seat for something. He emerges and looks not at Norma but into the corner of the garage where they've stashed a highway YIELD sign stolen in Ted's younger days. "She's my sister, Norm." Ted turns to face her. His eyes bug out. "My sister."

"My god."

"Yeah."

"Your dad's other—"

"Yeah."

It's not something they have often spoken of, and when he brings her up now Norma realizes how Ted has grown into being a fearful person and how she, Norma, has helped him do that.

"Have you met her before?" She gives Ted back dimensions he once had. Maybe he still has them. The possibility he might have a secret, be a secret. The possibility of kindness and depth, wonder, and maybe even grief.

"She came by my office today. Some friend of a friend of hers works there and told her that there was a Ted Jonsen in receiving. She just showed up. It freaked me out. She wants to borrow money. She scared the receptionist, so I told her to meet me here instead."

"She rode her bike. A little boy's BMX."

Ted nods. "She's my sister, Norm."

In the garage Norma finds a garden trowel. The day is already humid. She chooses a spot along the side wall. She'll dig. She'll plant as many trees as she goddamn wants. It's not like the universe cares if we are good or bad. She drives the trowel into the ground. A number of small roots cut across the cavity. Norma slices them with her trowel and they make a meaty sound. A bit of moisture collects on the severed cross sections. Norma pries a rock from the hole. She avoids the worms, minding not to cut their bodies in two.

Dirty Norma has followed her out. She stands beside her bike. She must have gotten the money from Ted.

Norma looks up to the sky. Reproducing is simply a matter of hormones. That's all. There's no judgment in it. It can happen to any asshole. Norma knows plenty of jerks who don't deserve their children. Her cousin Louis quizzes his kids whenever there's another adult around. "What are the heat panels on the space shuttle made out of? What birdcall is that? What are the three branches of the government?" She has only scratched the surface of the hole.

"You need help?" Dirty Norma asks.

But saying it's hormones is the same as saying witchcraft or sorcery. What's the difference between hormones and magic potions? Neither of them are believable or explainable.

Norma hands Dirty Norma the trowel. There's a spade on the deck. Reproducing is nothing more than making photocopies. Or plagiarism. It comes easily to cheaters. Norma finds the spade. She digs behind Dirty Norma. The day is warm. Then why does she want a baby so badly? She strikes the soil with her spade, balancing her feet on top of the dull end. Her actions are jerky and ineffective. The spade barely takes a bite. In the heat Norma can smell the fertilizer mix that her neighbor spreads on his lawn. She stops digging. She wants someone who belongs to her, someone she is a part of. It is plain and easy. It is tender.

Dirty Norma is much better at this digging than Norma. Maybe she's been in prison. She's really attacking the soil, making a difference. Norma looks at the ground to keep her balance, keep her head. It's a tiny hole she's dug. It's not much to ask for.

Norma's period is giving her cramps. She stares out across the yard, slowing the world down.

When they first moved in, the grass had been rolled out in strips of sod. It bothered Norma that first season. She could detect the edges of each roll, as if some night a lawn crew might return and roll the sod right back up again. Sometimes it is easy to hear what the grass is saying. To hear the message in the humming engine of the never-ceasing lawn mower five houses down.

A delivery truck backs up across the street. Norma focuses her attention on the head in front of her. Rage creeps in quietly, intimately, nearly unrecognized like a message whispered down a phone line made from paper cups and a string. In rage comes. Or it has been there a long while, sleeping. The afternoon opens up, awake now. The afternoon presents a notion Norma had not considered before: violence. She raises the spade above her head. *I could crack the blade into the thin bones of this woman's skull*, Norma thinks. *I could divide her like a worm, cut her into chunks, seeds I'd bury in the yard, planting baby trees. Trees that grow babies.* The choreography becomes clear. How the white brain will leak from inside Dirty Norma like moisture from a severed root. Red blossoms of blood flowering and a harvest of new humans come fall.

All around them are the small sounds of nature. Heat meeting green leaves, the sprinkler, the invisible bugs who are doing it in the grass, resilient now to pesticides, making babies in the yard. Norma tightens her grip on the spade's wooden handle. That dark head. The shovel's blade would lodge into the skull, then Norma would probably have to wiggle it free to take a second whack. In that moment of true horror, of committing true harm to another human's body, something would be exchanged, mingled, met. Something would be compensated. She'd give the world a reason for being so cruel to her. Norma still might never get a baby but at least she'd know why, and a reason would be something she could hold on to at night.

The strands of Dirty Norma's hair are separated into clumps. That head, one day a long time ago, popped out of some lady and the lady was happy to see it, happier than she'd probably ever been in her life. The lady drew the head up to her nose and smelled its black fur. She didn't care that the head was covered with scum and filth and blood. The lady dug her nose right down into the scent. That, or else Dirty Norma spontaneously sprung to life from some rotten idea.

The spade loses its bite. The delivery truck finds first gear and pulls away. Norma breathes, tasting the air's human scent, sweet as sweat. Soon, any minute now, she's going to put down this spade without injuring anyone.

A starling chirps. The world starts turning again. She looks down into the hole. It has gotten quite deep, deep enough to hold a tree if Norma only had one. She bites a ragged hangnail from her finger, chewing for a moment, then spitting it out into the hole. She plants a bit of herself, covering the hangnail with soil, replacing the sod as best she can, patting the lumpen mound.

ALL HANDS

Sweat makes a Rorschach blot on the back of my uniform. Coast Guard–issued poly-blended cotton never needs ironing but this shit does not breathe in Galveston's heat. Say the Gulf of Mexico is a stomach—we're stewing in the hypoxic dead zone. That means low oxygen, brown algae, and the curious side effect that boy fishes drown out the girls. I don't know why.

I take a bite of pizza, walking down the wharf to my office. I smell the crusty sea. I smell the burn of cargo cranes. Surrounded by giants. I smell gas and oil. The gulf's got twenty-seven thousand abandoned wells beneath its surface. I smell my dinner, warm comfort of grease. It smells delicious.

Last night I fell asleep at my desk. No tank ships or barges. No SARs to coordinate. I kept the radio up loud enough to wake me in case I needed to tuck in my shirt. *Semper paratus*. Sure. Sure. No such luck tonight.

The tankers that dock here to load are as big as entire towns, vacant city blocks. And taller still, solid walls of steel. I can make out a few letters on her side: CEAN IANT. She's empty, plenty of freeboard, taking on a load over at the facilities. I finish my meal, last bite of crust before stepping inside the trailer.

"Evening."

"Evening."

"When'd she get in?"

"Hour ago." Garza's a newish MIO. Nineteen, twenty. The local lady he's dating is waiting for him in the parking lot, pumping the AC in her Grand Am.

The wharves are vending machines for the local women. They select the option that suits their needs: a sailor in port for one or two shifts; a merchant marine who comes and goes on three-week rotations; or a coastie stuck in station for four long years. It's an easy arrangement I myself have enjoyed.

"You're the duty officer tonight?" he asks.

"No, ma'am." Sanctioned slang, pulling his chain. "Thought I'd skip down to Marine Safety for the all-night pancake breakfast." USCG-approved chuckles. "Care to hang around?"

"Hell, no. I've been here since oh eight hundred."

"You check her out yet?"

Garza winks. "I didn't want you to get bored through the wee hours."

"Thoughtful son of a gun."

Garza salutes like some feathered drum majorette and

disappears into a night that is dark, and hot, and filled with the chirping of insects.

The trailer quiets. My pizza slice has left a German shepherd–shaped grease stain on its paper plate. There's no denying that strange things happen in the state of Texas. I tack the dog/pizza plate up on my CO's corkboard. He's an animal lover. He also enjoys Italian foods. Always thinking toward promotion, yes I am.

I shove back out into the evening, hopping wharves over to the tanker.

"Permission to board?"

The ocean's dark as crude. No moon.

The reply sounds like "Permission granted, dork."

Tankerman's alone on deck. He's got a red kerchief tied round his neck and it suits him. A red neck. I've never seen this guy before, but it's simple: we don't like them; they don't like us.

I hear the ping and rattle of her hull getting charged. Dockman fills her. Pipes and pumps. She gurgles with gasoline. I try not to think of the girl I can't stop thinking of.

A full inspection takes two hours going by CFR standards. I start with the voids. My back's to the bulkhead and there's a planet's worth of ocean just outside, licking against the tanker, saying, *Don't mind me. Nothing happening here. Nothing except the metric tons of storm and riptide and killer sharks that the ocean runs with.* I check the welds for corrosion, fingering their lumpy seams. I don't like sharks. I check the pumps for leaks. Mostly, I don't even like the ocean. I check the emergency shutdown systems, listening to the ship, ticking off items on my checklist.

Is it dark inside her?

Check.

Is it scary?

It is.

Do I like it here?

I love it.

I think of the girl.

Check.

Six months ago she pulled a ten-dollar bill from her schoolbag as if she were going to pay me for services rendered. Her underwear rode up to cover her belly button. My boxers were the color of a Band-Aid. She'd stretched the bill between her hands like a proclamation. Sitting back down on my knee, she'd said, "He's so cute, isn't he?"

"Hamilton?"

"Uh-huh." Her eyes glazed, gaga over the bill. "Don't you just love him?" She rolled her heinie against my thigh.

"Hamilton?" I asked again.

Her answer was slow. "I call him Alexander."

A real patriot. I snaked my arm into her flabby abundance. "I'm more partial to this." I nibbled her shoulder. Her skin was soft and thin, like a frog's or a worm's, some gentle creature that grows mutated arms from its ears before the rest of us can even point to the source of the poison. A girl.

"Founding Father," she said, which made me feel creepy. I have a few years on her, four or five, but I don't want to be her daddy.

And there I was thinking her body and mind were

untroubled by the pursuit of popularity, untouched by the concerns prettier girls faced, while the whole time she's going straight to the top, dreaming on dead patriots.

She turned, eyed my federally issued shorts. "You ready for one more round? Just to make sure it worked?"

She was as fertile and plump as any field I'd ever plowed. She was also the first girl I'd ever met who actually wanted it to work. "No condom," she had said. "Once more. Just to be certain."

I liked this girl mostly because I couldn't understand a thing about her. I lay down, ready to serve my nation.

Tankerman and Dockman are still at it when I finish the inspection of the ship. On deck it's dark. Deck. Dock. Dork. Dark. Like a game of anagrams we played in Cape May. A few lights off the wharf leave the water thick, black, and bottomless. "You got a minute?"

Tankerman bristles and turns. Rough trade.

"I'm going to have to charge you with negligence. You know why?"

He shrugs, grabs his dick.

"You've got no flame screens on some of your vents. You've got product leaking into the water from the flange on the transfer hose. Can't you smell it spilling from the outboard flange? I don't need to tell you the kingdom come if you got flame in that tank."

The man lifts his eyebrows as a single ridge. That's all he's got to say. Like, *This job sucks.* Like, *I hate you coasties, anyway, and I could give a shit about product in the gulf.* He'll take the violation, slap on the wrist.

I pass him the ticket. "You'll need to appear before the ALJ. This has the date on it. Bring a copy of your COI and your Z-card. Got it?"

Tankerman grunts. Tankerman's a beast.

It's midnight under a skillet when I turn to leave. Wishing I had another slice of pizza and a flashlight. Wishing I could stop thinking about the girl and what I'd done. I reach for the wharf ladder without calculating how she's been loading gasoline for two hours. She's riding far lower and that ladder's not where I left it. Doesn't stop me from clawing and flailing and grabbing for it on my way down, down, down, falling between the barge and the wharf. Four or five stories, way too much time to consider the trouble I'm in. Like no PFD, like what my CO will have to say about that. I hit the sea and the smack knocks any lingering sense out of my head.

I'm underwater. After the first shock of being wet, heading deeper into the black sea, I remember what they taught us—kick off your shoes. I remember the girl, like maybe I deserve this. She was way too young. I swim to fight against the descent, to reverse it even, feeling all I don't know about the depth and darkness below me, the crush from above.

What's down there?

Twenty-seven thousand abandoned wells.

What else?

I couldn't say.

Isn't imagining worse than knowing?

Yes it is.

•

After we'd done it for the second time the girl had shown me her American history paper.

> Alexander Hamilton was born on the island of Nevis, on January 11 in either 1755 or 1757. He was illegitimate, meaning his mother, Rachel Faucette Buck, was not married to his father, James A. Hamilton. Still, Alexander became the first U.S. secretary of the treasury under George Washington. He established a national bank and a system of tariffs. He helped found the U.S. Mint and the Revenue Cutter Service, an outfit that would become the Coast Guard one day.
>
> Alexander Hamilton was a bastard.
>
> He was also a soldier in the Revolutionary War, the Whiskey Rebellion, and the Quasi-War.
>
> Hamilton married Elizabeth Schuyler. Then he cheated on her with Maria Reynolds. Hamilton resigned from office. Later on, he was shot by Aaron Burr in New Jersey. Later on, he died from his wounds in a house on Jane Street in New York City.
>
> The End.

D–. Her teacher had written across the top, *Where is your thesis statement? Where are your supporting paragraphs? This is your midterm American history paper, not some outline for a Wikipedia entry. This is unacceptable. Redo.*

"Is that why you chose me? Revenue Cutter Service?"

"Yup." She wasn't embarrassed to admit it.

"Shoot. A D-minus? That's 'cause you're a girl. I would have flunked you. That paper sucks."

"He's right."

"About what?"

"I did copy it from Wikipedia."

"Why?"

She chewed her cheek while she thought. "To establish the mediocrity democracy promotes." I could see a mole shaped like a mushroom at the base of her neck. "Just kidding. I did it 'cause no one's teaching me what I need to know."

"What's that?"

She studied me, bit her lip, but said nothing.

"Honey," I told her, jealous maybe, feeling cruel, "your boyfriend's been dead for decades."

I swim for the surface, though with no moon, there is no surface. I kick and flail, kick and pitch into the black water until I strike solid steel, and the full weight of the trouble I'm in arrives. I am under the ocean, under the hull of a half-loaded tanker. It is nighttime in America. In one direction there's air. In the other, miles of something else. Port and starboard are gone, replaced with a sudden memory of how I used to follow the path my father's tractor cut through some very tall grass, a green tunnel. I remember a grasshopper's weight bowing over a stalk of gama grass. My hands are on her hull, her heft. My lungs ache. She's huge. I cling to her underside, a lamprey, a remora. Inside, it's dry. Inside, air. I search her for a curve that might show the way back in, hoping she got whatever it was she wanted.

◆

Thirteen girls wait in the principal's office. Fourteen if you count me, the recording secretary. Though at forty, I'm not a girl anymore. And usually I'm just the regular secretary, but today there are legal concerns. Today we're official, so, recording secretary.

The scent of tropical fruit rises from the girls' hair. Their lotions and perfumes smell of the pharmacy. Better than the stale lunch on my breath. I stand. I sit. One pregnant teenager is a sight to catch your breath. Thirteen pregnant teenagers is an eclipse of sun, moon, earth.

"So."

There's a lot I could tell them. I was also pregnant in high school, a condition that ended in a Matamoros doctor's office. Or he said he was a doctor. I could tell the girls about that, if speaking intimately to the thirteen didn't feel like speaking intimately to Queen Elizabeth or the Virgin Mary. Though the Virgin Mary may be a bad example.

I verify the spellings of their names. "Meghan Collins? Meghan with an *h*?"

"Yes."

"Kristina Lepore? With a *K*?"

"Yes."

"Nancy Dean? That's easy."

Nancy smiles quickly, scared she's in trouble. I hear my office phone ring. It has been ringing ever since the girls started showing. Television, newspapers, national magazines. Parents wondering what we're doing.

"Amy England. Diane Nolan. Elizabeth O'Brien. Brien with an *e*. Lisa San—"

"—chez."

She volunteers before I can even get there.

"Sanchez. Of course. Katy Leese. Katy with a *K*? Leese with three *e*'s?"

"Right."

Each girl gets one moment of attention and a smile. I already know the proper spellings. I have their transcripts in front of me, but the room's so quiet I have to say something. "Well." I smooth the papers in my lap. "So. When are y'all due?"

Principal Caplan arrives. Principal Caplan has sweat in his sideburns. One pregnant teenager is a persimmon, odd but understandable. Thirteen of them is biting into a piece of molded fruit. Too ripe. Caplan's mouth opens. He takes his seat, hiding most of himself behind a formidable partner's desk. Principal Caplan has no partner. Neither of us does. Not really. My not-really boyfriend is a tankerman on the Gulf, so it's a life of dry spells when he's out at sea. Rumor is he's getting into port tonight, but he hasn't called yet.

Caplan looks like gray meat. We've been putting in twelve-hour days ever since pregnant teenagers started sprouting like fungi in our district. We're in one of those storms of media attention a person hears about. Everything awful and shrill and not from here is bursting down our doors, climbing in through the drainpipes.

Caplan stares at a stupid poster in his office that praises teamwork, that urges us to remember "Sticks in a bundle are unbreakable." He's too tired to know where to start with the girls. I cough to get him going, priming the pump, reminding him who is principal.

"Here's what I want to know," he says. I record his words in shorthand scribble. "Is this some sort of pact? A promise to raise the babies together?" He looks at each one of the girls with fatherly intention. "That's what they said on the news last night. Is that true, girls?" He clears spit from his lip edge. "I'm thinking it must be, because I know pregnancy's not contagious."

Hormones course past brains and ovaries. Lip balm and lonely slumber parties. Hot tears, humidly occult locker rooms, ringworm, and beige bra straps. Liz glances at the other girls' shoes. "Like, are we a coven of witches or something?"

Caplan tastes that idea. He nods his head. The man is stripped down to his bare nervous system, losing more of his comb-over every day. "Yes. Are you?"

Katy runs her hands across her belly. She's the largest. The skin is tight. She scratches and the other girls catch on, adding friction to their own bellies, basketing their fingers underneath to cradle the heft. All hands on deck. Caplan studies the roundness. Thirteen moons in the sky would be less surprising. He struggles to read the meaning in these bodies, like attempting braille for the first time. Frustration bugs his eyes out. Pregnancies as protolanguage, saying things the girls can't.

"No."

But what? And why can't the girls just say whatever they need to say? I give my own stomach a rub. Maybe they are too young to know what they need to say. Or maybe nobody taught them how.

Caplan slaps his hand on the desk. "Your parents are talking to lawyers and detectives. They're talking to your doctors. I just want you to tell me who did this to you."

Circled as wagons, the girls say nothing. Their toes twist. I tuck my face into the collar of my blouse, smell the fabric softener there. There's an insult confused with Caplan's question, making it clear how little he understands the girls in his care. They did this themselves. These bodies belong to them.

Caplan slaps his desk a second time and after a silence long enough to pour a cup of coffee in, he stands and opens his office door. He allows the district psychiatric counselor to enter. Caplan does not care much for Ellen. She wears turquoise jewelry. She used to be the drama coach but the town cut that program.

Ellen swoons and drops to her left knee in the midst of the thirteen. One pregnant teenager is a broken home. Thirteen pregnant teenagers is a Category 5 hurricane barreling toward Galveston.

Ellen asks the girls simple questions. "Do you eat breakfast? Have you seen a recent film?"

I record her words.

She asks, "Which subject in school is your favorite? What kind of music do you enjoy?" And then she asks, "Did you know that 'teen porn' is *the* most Googled search term on the Internet?"

The thirteen remain silent. Caplan boils. Ellen fingers her chunky bracelets.

"Really?" I ask. The room is so quiet. And all Ellen wants is to be able to talk to girls who won't talk. Ellen expands her gaze to include me. The girls bite their cheeks to not giggle. No one says a thing, so I have nothing to record. Ellen refreshes her face of anguish.

"Teen porn" floats in the room, flicking its fins.

It's hard getting old. Hard on a body, a mind, hard on a country. I formulate a fantasy of Ellen in a red, white, and blue negligee, clasping her chest like some neglected housewife, crying, *If it is porn they need, take me! Spare these young ones and use my forty-year-old, semiprecious body instead. Sub/dom, bondage? Fine. Facials, pee play? Horrors I'll endure to protect our young girls. Take me. Use me. I insist!*

Caplan breaks the quiet. "Thank you for your guidance, Ellen." He tries to excuse her.

But Ellen dusts off her slacks. "I'm not done yet." She stands with a hand on one hip. "Is it the law requiring a probe and a heartbeat that's preventing you from enjoying a normal high school experience?"

Caplan coughs wildly, as if by hacking loudly enough, he can travel a few seconds backward in time and erase the school's connection to the procedure Ellen has just suggested. Even if, privately, he'd counsel the same. This is Texas and he'd like to have a job in the morning, though the chances of that are getting slimmer and slimmer.

Some of the girls have polite smiles. Five of them check their cell phones in a chain reaction. Caplan gulps from a glass of ancient water on his desk until Amy or

Grace—I think it is Amy—finally asks, "Sir, may we be excused?"

Caplan stops gulping. I've never seen the man so sad. He stares at his hands as if they are now the size of paddles or tabletops—useless in the delicate work of raising children, braiding hair, tying shoelaces. Worse than useless—dangerous, bruising, deaf.

Caplan nods. Thirteen pregnant girls waddle their way out of his office. I plug in our hot pot for two more cups of coffee, but then I notice the last cup I made him untouched on his desk, cold. It's too much for one man, particularly one with old-fashioned ideas about protecting the children in his care.

With the girls gone, like some sort of palate cleanser or smelling salts, Caplan allows himself to watch a YouTube video of Jerry Lee Lewis pounding away on a poor Baldwin.

"I love him," Caplan says. "I love the Killer. Just look at him."

I was never a huge fan. That business with the cousins and the dead wives. But together we watch "Crazy Arms" and "What's Made Milwaukee Famous." Jerry Lee's up. He's down. His fingers look like jumping spiders covered with gaudy gems big as babies' fists. He plays piano with one foot on the keys. He plays piano with his elbows.

"Someday the only reference to us in the newspaper will be the field hockey scores."

"Absolutely." I try to cheer Caplan with a smile.

He switches off his monitor. "There are reports of three girls in Boling-Iago and five in Manvel. The governor's calling me in the morning."

"The governor? Why?"

"He wants someone to blame."

"For every pregnant teen in Texas?" I hadn't thought of that angle yet, a contagion, airborne spores we propagated.

Caplan follows something outside the window. "It's not my fault."

"Of course it's not."

He lifts his head, looking like a boy, asking permission. "I'm taking the afternoon off, okay? I need to think about what I'm going to tell the governor."

"Good idea."

Principal Caplan grabs his windbreaker from the coatrack and blows a raspberry as goodbye on his way out.

The files on my desk are stuffed to bursting. I touch the newspaper clippings and the sweetly scented insurance forms. There are op-eds and PTA minutes in which concerned community members blame Gardasil, high-fructose corn syrup in cafeteria lunches, loose relationships with biological fathers, Democrats, yoga, Republicans, dioxin-steeped feminine products. In all that paper, all those words, the girls say nothing. And I suppose that is the point.

◆

The quiet of afternoon nature films pervades the hallways. At the end of a long row of lockers the thirteen gather together undisturbed. With the sun just so, buffed circles of wax are visible on the vinyl flooring. The girls speak softly, huddled in a whirlpool. The light is full of dust particles.

One asks the others, "Have your feet swelled? None of my shoes fit anymore."

"No, but I haven't pooped in weeks."

A round of giggles.

"And all this extra spit in my mouth. How come no one ever told us about that?"

Four girls shake their heads, knowing so little about the pregnant body, about American history, about life after pregnancy when stares of wonder turn to pity, disgust.

One mentions the tenderness of her breasts as she lifts off the ground. Words slip from lips; the current gently eddies. The girl in the air is joined by two others, floating, balloons. They glow, lanterns above, more and more girls still, until the last one, full of grace, so round, leaves her tiptoes and lifts off the linoleum. In the air, the girls dip and reel. One turns giddy somersaults. Weightless, swimming. "Woo," she might say. "That feels good." Big as stars. Beautiful as a poisoned sunset and just as far out of reach.

"Anybody's gums bleeding?" one asks.

"When I brush my teeth."

"What about your ankles?"

"Take a look." Five others breaststroke over to Liz's feet. "Like elephants'!"

More giggling.

"Nothing's the way I expected it would be," one girl says. "It's like, you know, when you're talking on the phone and suddenly you can't remember a word? You wait for the word to come, feeling it on your tongue. Yeah. I feel this little life, little death floating nearby. I just can't say it yet."

"Yeah," the others answer. "Sure. Sure thing."

"And this part"—Annie spreads her arms, the wonder, the weightlessness—"is the weirdest part of all."

"Except for growing a tiny human inside your body."

"Yeah. That's pretty weird, too."

"Anyone else still puking?"

A door slams down the hallway. Milkweed seeds in hoopskirts, the girls fall back to the ground.

"No. But French fries are still the only thing I can really eat."

◆

Eventually my non-boyfriend calls. His tanker's come in. He says he'd like to see me.

Caplan's been gone awhile now, so I collect my things. I've done my duty. I finger the nameplate on Caplan's desk, hoping it will still be there in the morning. He doesn't deserve to lose his job. It's not his fault alone. Adolescent girls can be hard to understand. They are like an uncontacted tribe of humans. And maybe they should remain that way. Maybe we should collect all the adolescent girls in America and send them out to sea together. Eventually the rest of us would miss them so much we'd try harder to understand why they are the way they are and why we think such awful things about them. We'd realize how scared and wrong we'd been to think girls are made only of light things.

I head down to the water to meet my sailor. At the edge of the wharf I'm terribly small under the twilight sky, next to this much industry. For one moment I turn back. I wonder, What if the pregnant girls followed me here? What if they flowed behind me, streams, beautiful daughters, rivers making their way to the sea? And what if the flood of girls doesn't stop at the water's edge as I have? What if the girls, with the help of several strong longshoremen, load themselves onto an armada of waiting tankers, barges, ships, and tugs? What if they leave us? Poor King George without his colonies. What if they leave the land barren? I imagine the girls waving goodbye, trailing streamers, scarves, a few tears. Not just the thirteen, but all of them, all girls, everywhere. Hundreds, thousands, millions of girls. And what if I don't stop them? What if the Coast Guard does nothing to guard the coast? What if I even patted the hulls on their way out into the gulf because I'm not sure we deserve girls yet? "Take care," I might say. "See you."

"When?" A fifteen-, maybe sixteen-year-old, would want to know.

I'd shrug. Who can say how long it will be before the rest of us understand girls? Deserve them? How long until it is safe.

"Okay," she'll say. "Okay." She isn't scared of anything. She's off to populate new lands, a redo.

It's terribly quiet by the water, and in the quiet it's awful to know what it would sound like if, or once, the girls, our girls, leave us. Once they all harden up into non-girls.

Which really is just foolish thinking. It's only quiet because the girls are home having dinner with their families, watching television in order to learn the popular ways of love.

My not-really boyfriend arrives with a sixer. He's been in for hours, he says, nearly loaded. Clearly, this is a booty call. With the beer in hand we steal down the ladder onto the tanker. I've been here before, or on others just like this one. Big as hell and half of Texas. The ships seem too large to be man-made. Each step disorients me, because if men didn't build them, what did? Monsters? Magicians? I just don't know.

He wraps one arm around my shoulders. He's greasy. That's fine, comes with the job, a tankerman skilled in handling natural resources. We drink on the deck, kissing, fooling around, tiny things. Then we drink some more, stare out to sea.

"I can't stop thinking about those girls," I say.

"You can't protect them."

"Why not?"

"Well, what are you protecting them from? Boys?"

"No."

"Then what?" He drives his thumb into his chin. "They're not special. They're girls. They're not pure." He rubs his head, scratches the grime there.

I tuck my knees, cross my ankles. "I know."

He keeps on. "They're doing the strongest thing they can think of. Murder, death—that's easy. Birth? Not easy." The loading ship gurgles. He pats my back. Sometimes he's smart. "Your girls are just taking a nine-month dip into the infinite. They'll be back in PE before graduation rolls around." He lifts his bottle of beer and tips it to me. "Sounds like she's just about full. Let me go check on the load and then we can get out of here. 'Kay? Half hour tops, 'kay?"

"Where are we going?" I ask, but he's already gone and I already know. My bed, fast as we both can get there. Thank god.

There's a rainbow in a puddle on deck. Oil or gas. Pink and blue and green shining in the pier lights. I stamp my foot in the puddle. I haven't eaten since breakfast. Half an hour? Unlikely. It'll take him longer than that to finish. I decide to acquaint myself with the galley.

Belowdecks I unlatch cabinets, poke around. I find a sailor's small photo album. Pictures of siblings, some children on a green, green yard. I find a letter from home about painting pinecones with peanut butter and birdseed. I find some chocolate and English muffins. I turn to toast the muffins, and when I turn round again, a coastie, dripping wet and barefoot, is standing in the open hatchway. His stubble has some red in it, but he's not tall, not threatening. He's the sort of man a girl will look at and think, *That's cute, that's some mother's son. A good kid.* His eyes are open wide, as if he's been listening to ghost stories.

"You scared me. I thought everyone was gone," I say. He's drenched. "You need a towel?"

"Thank you." He comes into the kitchen.

I find a stack of clean dish towels in a small hutch. "What were you doing? Swimming?"

"I fell in."

"Tonight? In the dark?"

He nods.

"Holy cow. That's scary."

He buries his face in a dry towel.

"You need some tea? Something to warm you up?"

"No thank you, ma'am." He drapes the towel over one shoulder, stares at something, not me. "I was under the ship."

"What a nightmare. You're lucky to be alive."

"Yeah." He looks at his pruned hands as if they might bite him.

"Have some tea. Or water."

He looks up. "All right," he says. "Okay, water."

I fill a glass. "How long were you under there?"

"I don't know. A long time."

"How'd you get out?"

"I felt where her belly curves. Followed the curve up. Found the pilot's ladder on her side."

"I think you need a doctor." The man must be in shock. "I'll call an ambulance." I pull out a chair for him to sit on. "What's your name?"

He reaches his hands into the pockets of his uniform as if he might find his name there. He pulls out a wad of bills, money, soaking wet. "I'm Coast Guard. SIO," he says. "Do you work here?"

I'm still wearing my pumps and skirt suit. No doubt there's some maritime law restricting girlfriend access on a twenty-thousand-deadweight tanker that's taking on a load of gasoline. And I'm not really even a girlfriend. "No. I work at the high school."

The coastie tenses up, an electric current entering his wet body. He nods. He looks at me and I understand: I am breaking some Homeland Security law. I try to explain. "I was just bringing my guy dinner, just dropping it off. I'm leaving now. Right now."

"The high school?"

"Yeah."

"Where all the girls are pregnant?"

"Yeah."

He stuffs the bills back in his pocket. "How are those girls doing?"

My voice is flat and annoyed. I shake my head. "They're great. Yeah. Sure. Healthy."

"Sounds like you're mad at them."

"They're a lot of extra work for me." I'm not mad. I'm just tired of trying to figure out what the girls mean.

"Must be something, standing in the same room as them."

"They were in my office today."

He pales. "That right? What'd they say?"

"Not much."

"Thirteen of them?"

I shrug. "It happens."

"No, it doesn't. Not really."

I fill his water glass again. "No. I guess not."

"So. Why'd they do it?" Like he's running an inspection. Like he somehow thinks I'll know the answer.

When I was a girl I pretended my pillow was a different man each night. And the pillow men would take me here, or there, out into life, to a Bee Gees concert maybe. That seemed like an adult thing to do. Men made the weather and I loved them for it. Then I got pregnant, then the real men disappeared, and I made my own weather. Storms. Sunshine. Storms. I blow air up my face, faking exasperation. "I couldn't say."

There's a pool of water beneath his chair.

"You were under the ship?"

He nods.

"Let me call an ambulance."

"No, thanks. XO's gonna kill me as it is."

"You've got no shoes."

"I'll be all right." He returns the towel he used and backs his way out of the galley.

I follow him up to the deck. From the gangway he throws one arm into the air, a goodbye. His hand makes a bird in the night. He'd be a nice one, I think. Make some girl happy. "What's your name?" I shout, but he has already crossed back over to the wharf, leaving nothing but the damp stains of his footfalls.

My guy takes way longer than half an hour. Black ripples obscure the view, but that doesn't stop me from staring into the water. It's thick as oil, dark as glass, and I've got time to wonder how long that coastie was under, to wonder what's down there.

One by one, round lights dot the surface of the sea like fireflies or lampposts just coming on, or something else maybe, colonies, mothers, boats heading to far-off places. I don't know what the lights are. I can't say if they're coming from above the water or underneath. Golden circles float across the ocean surface as if the full moon rose while I was belowdecks. Only there isn't one moon. There's a grand chandelier, ten moons, then thirteen, ten more, thirty-two, one hundred and eight, seven thousand and six moons—an entire language made up of moons floating over the surface of the sea.

Can the coastie see this phosphorescence? Does he understand what the girls mean or does he, like me, at least understand that he doesn't understand? We don't know the alphabets they use, but we can read a curve. We see a girl's reflection. We tilt our faces toward their glow, warmed by their light, their meaning bubbling up from a dark sea.

BEAST

I read the newspaper in bed at night, propping it open on my belly. My boobs fall off to either side as if they are already asleep. They care little for the news of the world after the day is done. Still, I read the paper as a refreshment, like a breath mint or a catalog filled with clothes I would never buy.

On page eighteen of the *National Report* there's an article, "Good Guy Gets the Chicks." It's the story of a brother who works at a chicken rendering plant by day and at a security firm by night in order to send his sister to college. He sells his plasma to make ends meet.

He must be Japanese or Amish. I flip ahead to the jump page to see his picture. He's just some white guy from Minnesota, and I guess I find that hard to believe. He's like an artifact from the nineteenth century, back when people still took turns churning the butter or tending fires at night. In the photo he's wearing sneakers and a plastic apron stained with blood. He's positioned along a conveyor belt that is dotted with the dead bodies of chickens. He's from right now.

"Archibald Lepore never finished high school," the article says, "yet every month he sends the Student Loan Corporation a check for $578. Mr. Lepore has been working since he was sixteen years old to support his twin sister. He found a second job when they turned eighteen and she was admitted to Northwestern University without a scholarship. Mr. Lepore, from the refrigerated storeroom of PoulTech, says—"

But then it moves. Just slightly. "A tick," I tell my husband. A tiny black dot with legs. A period, escaped from the newspaper, is making a slow-motion dash across my stomach.

"Another one?" My husband rolls onto his side. "Let me see."

"Right here."

He moves in for a closer look. "That's a pimple you picked."

"I wasn't picking anything. I was just reading. It's a tick. Do you see it?"

He spreads the skin of my stomach. "There's a spot of blood."

"Any legs?"

"I don't see anything really."

"Deer ticks are very small."

"I know." It's my third tick this week. "But I don't see anything." He pauses over the spot, exhales. "Wait. All right. Wait. I see something."

"What?"

"Squirming a little bit. Black."

I knew it. "Pull it out."

"You're not supposed to pull them out. Then the head stays inside."

We had received an illustrated mailer from the county. "Lyme Tick Awareness." *The sickness is carried in their saliva*, it said. *Get the head out.*

"What am I supposed to do?"

He disappears into the bathroom for some tweezers and a cotton ball soaked in alcohol.

The cottage we live in is only one story and a bit run-down. It's what's called a carriage house. It's on someone else's property. We are caretakers. We mow the lawn, handle the trash, look out for robbers and all that. That's how we manage to live here, a place crawling with deer and mice and ticks, instead of in an apartment in town. At this hour, from our bedroom, the rest of the house feels dark and dangerous. Things might be creeping, rotting, plotting revenge out there and I wouldn't even know because I can't see the living room, and beyond that I can't see the small kitchen with two windows that look out onto a screen porch that looks out even farther onto the road and the mailboxes. I can't see any of that right now.

"Have you been rolling around in the grass?" He dabs at the spot and I can smell the astringent. He clamps down with the tweezers. "Ready?" He yanks once, taking a bit of skin with it. "That ought to do it." He applies the alcohol.

I don't know if he pulled the head out. His mouth is twisted, worried.

"Is it gone?"

"Yeah. You're fine."

"Sure?"

"I'll look again in the morning."

"What if the morning is too late?"

"You're fine." He takes the tweezers and whatever he's tweezed back to the bathroom. I hear the toilet flush and see him walk through the living room. He has on a pair of boxers and a ribbed undershirt. When we were teenagers my husband worked in Akron's rubber plants. Now most of those plants are gone and he found a job running the heavy machinery for, oddly enough, a heavy machinery manufacturing center. He's still very strong. He still has the figure of a man who grew up lugging around one-hundred-pound tires all day. We went to high school together and married a few years after we graduated. I am lucky. I made a good decision by accident. In high school we chose boyfriends blindly, pin the tail on the donkey. I thought he was handsome and that was about all I thought. So I was surprised to find, after we'd been married a few years, that my husband was someone I really love. There are things about him he'd kept hidden in school, secrets that made him precious—kindness and wonder and a beautiful singing voice—qualities that took a couple of years of life chipping away before they were revealed.

"Can you take off your clothes?" I ask when he returns.

"I like my pajamas."

"Those aren't pajamas. They're underwear."

"Not necessarily."

He takes off his clothes anyway and looks at me once

as if I were a brand-new flashlight whose bulb, for some reason, has already dimmed and malfunctioned. But I'm not brand-new. We've been married for almost eleven years now.

He gets back into bed. I wrap my body around the tick bite. I can see the picture of the chicken-rendering brother from Minnesota. He smiles up at me from the floor where I dropped him. I have a sister. She'd never work at a chicken plant for me. I also had a brother once. I don't think he would have done it either. Not because he wasn't kind, and not because he was busy with his own plans. He didn't have any plans. My brother had trouble knowing what to make of his life. There were days he'd feel inspired by a Tony Robbins infomercial or something stupid and he'd think, *Well, maybe I should get a job,* as if that were something no one else had ever considered before. A job. But then my brother never could hold down any sort of position except for a few short stints at a dry cleaner in town. He reminded me of Abraham Lincoln, so tall he stooped his head, pockmarked, peach-fuzzed, and as quiet as jewelweed before it explodes. When he graduated from high school he froze, caught in the headlights, distracted by every leaf on every tree. He couldn't move forward because he couldn't see the point of it. "Don't you know where forward is headed?" he asked one Thanksgiving. I didn't have an answer. He scratched his ear. He stared out the window of our parents' house as if there might be an answer in the drive. I don't think he saw anything. He sat back down and stared at the carpeting. Maybe I should have said something. I know where forward is headed. I try not to think about it.

We didn't find him for three days because we didn't realize he was missing. That's the saddest part of this story. He'd hanged himself from a tree, one of several that grew in a small sliver of land between my parents' house and the neighbors', out by a swing set untouched for years. He timbered over like a sapling when my father cut him down, his body gone stiff. Afterward, my mother, a stone-faced woman, a hard worker, kept repeating a phrase as if it were the motto of my brother's suicide. "He was just too in love with the world." She said it to everyone.

"You know *The Pajama Game*?" I ask my husband, my mouth close to the side of his chest. "The musical?"

"No."

"Yeah, you do. It's old. Has that song 'Hernando's Hideaway.' "

"No."

" 'Just knock three times and whisper low that you and I were sent by Joe'?"

"Oh. Yeah. Yeah."

"I never understood what they were doing inside Hernando's Hideaway."

"Hmm." His eyes are closed.

"So what were they doing?" I ask.

"What?" He opens his eyes.

"Inside Hernando's Hideaway?"

"What were they doing? I don't know. Drinking, dancing, fooling around. Adult things."

"Yeah, that's it. Adult things. That's why it was scary."

"You were scared of a song?"

"That song. There was something going on inside that club, something criminal."

"I don't know."

"I do."

"Then what was it?"

"Like you said. Adult things."

"What's that?"

"Well, what's the most adult thing?"

"Fucking?"

"No. Fucking's for kids. Dying is adult."

"Oh. Shhhh," he says and turns to rub my face. He puts his hand on my cheek to stop my jaw from moving. He doesn't want to hear about how people were dying inside that song's nightclub. That that was the reason they kept the security so tight. My husband gets nervous if I say anything too bizarre. He thinks I might also end up swinging in the breeze one day. But I used to say bizarre things even before my brother died. And I don't think suicide is contagious. "Shhh, baby," he says one more time before shutting off the light.

I've been having a really strange week.

"Honey?" I ask once the lights are out. He mumbles, trying to sleep. I tuck the covers around my chin and close my eyes, thinking it won't happen if I can just go to sleep fast enough. But this week I haven't been able to fall asleep quickly. I know it's coming, so I fret and listen while my husband's breath deepens and slows. My chest gets tight and small. My eyes go dry. Once he is asleep the night changes. I hear every sound and every sound is scary. The furnace, the frogs, the cable wire scraping against the roof. The more alone I get, the louder the world becomes. There are wild animals outside, raccoons, squirrels, skunks, possums. I listen and then I try to brace myself, holding on to the sheets. I know it's coming, a dream of a tidal wave. I get ready for it. I wait, and just when I think too much time has passed, that maybe it won't happen tonight, it happens, so quickly I can't scream. My hands and feet harden into small hooves, the fingers and toes swallowed up by bone, and then the most frightening part is over with, the part where I lose my opposable thumbs. Next the fur, brown speckled with some white. This sprouting feels like a stretch or like I'm itching each individual follicle from the inside as a wiry hair pokes through a pore. My arms and legs narrow, driving all their muscles up the flank. My neck thickens and grows. I feel my tail. I like my tail. Finally my face pulls into a tight, hard nose. My jaw extends, my tongue grows long and thick, my lips shrink before turning black and hard as leather. And then it's done. And then I am a deer.

I still haven't told my husband, but I practice telling him. "Lately," I imagine saying, "when you turn out the light, something funny happens to me."

"What?" I think he'll ask, or just, "Funny? What do you mean?"

"I turn into a deer at night." I plan on telling him clearly like that, no hemming, no mistaking what I mean.

"A deer?" He won't believe it. I know he won't.

"A deer," I'll confirm.

"What the fuck?" he'll say, just like that. "What the

fuck?" with a slowness that means he's thinking hard about what I'm saying.

"Calm down," I'll tell him. Though he'll probably be calm already.

"What are you talking about?" he'll ask me, disappointed, as if he already knows deer don't mate for life.

I am very careful, very quiet, planting my hooves on our bed. I stand over him, staring down at his body from up on my wobbly legs, straddling his belly. I sniff his neck, licking the hair of his armpit, cleaning him. Though I don't want to wake him, I kind of can't help it. I don't know what would happen if he woke up now. He keeps a .22 and a shotgun in the hall closet.

When I was growing up the land around here was different. Mostly there were a lot of soybean farms, hog farms, and wide, wide tracts of government-owned land where every now and then you'd see men digging with bright lights late at night, looking for natural gas. Sometimes the gas diggers would wake me up when I was a girl. Their lights were so bright it was easy to imagine they were coming from an alien's spaceship. The gas-well sites were all connected by long straight roads on the government land. These roads went on forever and, driving down them, it became easy to imagine the roads were closing up behind my parents' car, sealing us in. No one could follow us. Or no one else existed. My brother, sister, and I would stare out the back window watching where we'd once been disappear.

It's not like that anymore. As soon as they didn't find

much gas, the government sold the land off to developers, makers of strip malls.

When we were young, there was a man named Pete who lived around here. Pete kept a wild deer as a pet. Everyone said that Pete had done things with the deer, though I don't see how they could know that. It was a small town. Rumors spread. Soon people started saying even more. They said that Pete had done things with his own daughter also, and there might have been some truth to that. She had been taken away by the state. People didn't know why but they guessed why. The spookiest part of the whole story, and the reason people suspected him, is because Pete named the deer after his daughter, Jennifer. He'd call the deer, "JENNIFER. JENNIFER." You could hear him at night. "JENNIFER. JENNIFER." Slowly. And the deer would come when called, as if it were a dog and not a wild creature. She'd come to him.

I've been thinking about Pete lately, about how messed up people are by sex, by other people, because despite his failings as a human being—I liked Pete. He knew a lot about the woods, about nature. He knew which kind of mushrooms you could eat and which would kill you. He collected the old seed pods of water chestnuts. They looked like hard black stars. He told me when deer are young they have no scent. That way, before the deer can walk, their mothers can hide them in the tall grass, and as long as the mother goes away, no predators will find the babies. Some divine plan. Almost. Pete found Jennifer when she was just a fawn. He'd stumbled onto her in a field. Her mother must have been killed by a construction truck, because the fawn was about to die from hunger. She'd been waiting in the tall grass but her mother didn't return and so Pete found the fawn, picked her up, carried her home, and made her a bottle of milk. He raised her in his barn after he lost his own daughter to the state. And then, when the deer was old enough, the rumor was that he treated the animal in a similar manner.

Eventually I fall asleep and, when I wake in the morning, I am a woman again. My husband is just starting to move, making a smacking noise with his lips.

Maybe Pete just thought, *Well, I'm no better than this deer, am I?* I don't know what happened to the deer, but Pete is dead now so I feel like I can say it here under the covers with my husband still asleep: I always thought there was something romantic about the way he named the deer after his daughter. Even if it was messed up.

When I tell my husband what is happening to me at night, which I'm going to do, very soon now, he'll want to know how, and then, after that, he'll want to know why I am becoming a deer. That's the most troubling part and the reason I'm having trouble telling him.

"My name's Erich. With a *ch*," clarifying.

I thought: *He is lying because liars use detail. Married*, I thought, and I was annoyed he would lie so I told him my real name. I even told him where I worked. I even told him I was married.

When, later that night, my husband asked, "Did you

have fun with the girls? What'd you all end up doing?" I used details. I told him we went to Akron, to a new, fancy nightclub that had a bouncer at the door and a velvet rope. I told him Sarah bumped into a cocktail waitress carrying a tray of three drinks. I told him Vicky had been getting religious lately. And I told him Meghan had gone out on a date with Steve Perry, the singer from Journey. I told him she said Steve Perry was nice, but the whole time she couldn't stop singing, "Don't stop! Believin'!"

"Sounds good," my husband said. "Steve Perry. That's cool."

In an evening filled with that many details there wouldn't have been time for me to meet Erich, or whatever his name was, in the line for the bathroom. There wouldn't have been time for him to follow me into the ladies' room, where, with his hand up my shirt, he started biting my neck and chest like he was lost in some fever, like he was going to eat me with his lips that were thick and filled with blood.

"I'm going to call in sick to work," I tell my husband.

"You don't feel well, hon?"

"No. I'm fine. I just can't go to work today."

In the living room, I call my boss. It's early enough that I can just leave a message. "You've reached Sachman's Real Estate Agency. No one is here to take your call. Kindly leave your name, number, and a brief message and one of our agents will get back to you. Thank you."

I tell her I have Lyme disease. I tell her I won't be coming in. I cough into the phone and say goodbye. I get back in bed. The cough might have been overdoing it.

My husband is getting ready for work. He's wearing socks, boxers, a T-shirt, and a flannel. He comes into the bedroom eating a bowl of cereal, looking for his pants and shoes. "You don't feel well?" he asks again.

"I feel fine."

"Then why are you staying home from work?"

I stare at a blank spot above our bureau. "I hate it there."

"You do?" He's surprised.

"I started to yesterday."

"Oh."

He shakes his head. I lie back in the bed. I hear him open his dresser drawer. He has arms and legs that move perfectly. He pulls ticks off me. He came from his mother and nothing is wrong with him. He went to elementary school, where probably, one day, someone wasn't nice to him. Maybe they called him jerk. Under the covers, I hate these kids who might have said that to him because I didn't mean to cheat on him. It was an accident like a car crash. Except I'd tell him if I had crashed the car.

I pick up the paper from off the floor where I dropped it last night. Insurgents and Rebels. Genocide and Corporate Malfeasance. American box stores in Manchuria. Manatees in Florida. I open to the center spread. It looks a bit like the periodic table of elements. The photos are tiny, crammed onto the page. The images of all the local soldiers killed last year. The dead stare out from their enlistment photos or senior high school portraits. They're arranged alphabetically. They are young. Some soldiers share similar last names, as if entire families were wiped out, but of course they're not family. They probably didn't even know one another. Anderson. Brown. Clark. Davis. DeBasi. Green. Hall. Kern. All those young people and all my head can think about is what I've done and all my body wants is to do it again.

Erich's lips surprised me because how could someone new, someone I'd just met in a bar, have spit that tasted familiar? They were a little salty like we'd all really come from the ocean once. Huge lips and watery eyes. That's about all I ever dreamed. Erich told me, like a cut in my ear, "I'd fuck you to death," and for the past five days I've been hearing him say that over and over again. Touching the scab. "I'd fuck you to death. I'd fuck you to death." Each time it feels like getting punched in the stomach, only lower, deeper than the stomach, like I can't breathe in my legs. Then for the past five nights I've been turning into a deer.

The phone starts to ring. It is probably my sister. I lie in bed listening to the ring.

When my sister had her second baby a couple of months ago I told her, "That's weird."

"What is?"

"You just made another death in the world."

"Fuck off," she said. I guess she thought I was referring to our brother.

"All right," I told her. "Okay." But she's been a little angry at me ever since. She's been a little mean, as if I were responsible for the fact that we all have to die sometime.

My husband and I both just let the phone ring. It's too early, and soon enough, after five rings, it stops. I hope it wasn't my boss calling me back.

I'll tell him. Any minute now I'll say it. "Imagine what it's like to lose your opposable thumbs, to have them bone up into hard hooves. It was scary at first," I'll say. "How do you think deer open doors?"

"I don't know. How?" He'll imagine I'm telling him a joke.

"They don't."

If I tell him, maybe he can build a special door for me. He's handy like that. A door that doesn't require opposable thumbs. Still, he'll want to know where I'm going at night. And what would I say? Out with the other deer? He wouldn't like that. The deer around here have been forced out into the open by the new construction. They get hit by cars all the time. He won't want me to go out with the deer. So where would I go? Back to the nightclub? The bouncer would be surprised to find a deer trying to enter a club as nice as his, but he'd let me in. "It takes all kinds," he'd say, throwing open a velvet curtain on the room. Just knock three times and whisper low. The song says something about castanets and silhouettes. I'd scan the nightclub for Erich. Couples would sit around small cocktail tables snapping their fingers in time to the rhythm of the song. A scent would hit me and I'd turn into it just like a movie star slapped across her face. Beautiful with a fever. I'd rev my hoof across the dance floor. I'd smell thick lips. I'd smell the blood of an animal the kitchen staff's preparing. I'd lick my lips, slowly, letting my pink tongue dangle out of my black mouth a little just like some animal waiting by the side of the road for the driver who killed it to come back one more time and kill it again.

•

I sit up in bed and spread out the skin of my stomach. The hole the tick made swelled up into a bead, a pink bead of skin, like some new growth. I pick at it but it is hard and I can't get much purchase. I rest the tip of one finger on the spot, as if my finger is a stethoscope. I try to hear what is happening underneath. There is something going on, a rumbling. Maybe he didn't get the head out. It's not his fault. It's hard to get the head out and he's squeamish when it comes to hurting me. Even when I ask him to.

"I wonder if I have Lyme disease," I finally say to him, but this is actually a minor fear, a made-up fear compared with what I am really thinking about: my tail, my hooves. He turns to look at me. I try again. "I mean, I've been thinking a lot about deer." He has a seat beside me on the bed, raising his eyebrows. But that is not quite what I mean, and so this time I try to be honest with my husband. I say it. "I mean, I think I'm becoming a deer."

"You think you're becoming a deer?" he asks.

Erich called me at work yesterday to tell me what he wanted to do to me. He said he wanted to see me. He said he wanted to eat my roast beef pussy. One thing very general, one thing very specific. It made it difficult for me to breathe hearing those very specific words. No one had ever said that combination of things to me before. I was shocked by how powerful those words were. I started to think that maybe he actually wanted to kill me. Thus, the reference to beef. Thus, "I'd fuck you to death."

After he hung up I thought about Becky and Tom

Sawyer in the cave, though I haven't read that book in twenty years. I don't think Tom would ever talk that way to Becky. And I couldn't actually remember what happened to them down in the cave or why they were there, but danger was nearby and Tom was keeping Becky safe. There were bad men in the cave, bad men who filled the cave with the stench of their badness. I bet Becky could smell it. I bet it made her think differently about Tom. Maybe she would have been interested to hear the things those bad men wanted to do to her.

This morning I can see through the living room into the kitchen. I can see the mailboxes waiting by the edge of the road. Lust makes room, the way a bomb exploding makes room, clearing things out of the way. I listen for a moment, trying to position my ear near my heart. I can't get my head very close. *Tickticktickticktickticktick.* I don't actually hear any bombs ticking. I'm just worried for my husband.

"You're becoming a deer?" he asks me again.

My husband is looking out the window. He is wincing. Maybe he is thinking about something else, something that happened at the heavy machinery plant, maybe he is thinking about another woman, perhaps one we knew in high school who didn't have problems like this.

We sit in silence. I don't want to say anything more just yet. I want, for a moment, to let it be.

"Will you show me?" he asks and doesn't wait for an answer before telling me what to do. "Show me."

That's not what I had thought he'd say.

"Okay," I answer very quietly. "I will tonight."

"A deer," he says.

"A deer," I repeat.

"All right," he says. "All right," and then he leaves without kissing me goodbye.

"Bye," I yell.

He grabs his coat and the front door slams shut, not because he's angry but because the wood has swollen and in order to get our front door to shut one has to slam it closed. Or maybe he is also angry and he is just disguising his slamming in the swollen door.

I stay home while he's at work, as if I really am sick. In the bed I feel something foreign bloom between my husband and me, an intruder, a mold. I see my husband with eyes that don't know him, as if he quite suddenly became a man from Brazil, or grew a beard, or started speaking in a southern accent. As if after eleven years of marriage he somehow had all of his secrets returned to him, made secret again.

We don't talk about it at dinner or even after dinner when we're watching TV, brushing our teeth. Instead he tells me a story about a guy at work who'd been running a credit card scam and got caught. "You never would have suspected this guy," he says. "Older fella, balding and stooped. He didn't seem smart enough. He didn't seem like he cared enough about being rich to become a criminal."

I climb in bed to read the paper, but can't concentrate on the words there. The nervousness inside me is messing with my thoughts, getting ready to blow. The newspaper says something about the Peking Opera, something about a volcano in Indonesia, something about a government cover-up, but it's all the same to me.

My husband has stopped talking. He takes off his clothes without my even asking him to and stands in front of me, pulling on one ear like there's an honesty tonight, a bright rawness I'd never seen before. He is beautiful to look at. I slide the newspaper to the floor and he shuts off the light. We don't say good night to each other. I'm too nervous. We don't say anything, and the air is rigid between us in the dark. I wait, blinking my eyes, seeing nothing. I worry. There's no guarantee anything will happen. Just because something has happened doesn't mean it will continue to happen and then he will think I'm crazy and then he will call some girl we knew in high school, one who doesn't have problems like this. One who doesn't have a dead brother. I listen for him to fall asleep, for his breath to change, but it doesn't. Instead he clears his throat. I hear him stay awake, imagining his eyes blinking open against the dark like mine. I wait and wait, listening. America at night, a couple of cars, some wind, a plane overhead, a blue jay or a crow— one of the birds with an ugly voice is upset about something outside. I wait and listen until I can't wait any longer. The blanket is up around the back of my neck. My eyes shut as a woman, and I am asleep before it happens.

When I wake it is still night. I can tell because there is a small knot of unknown fear in my lungs and a soupy proximity to every memory I've ever had. Something is rousing me, something wants for attention. A poke, a sharpness dragged across the fur of my back. I seize up the muscles in my neck. The barrel of a gun.

Though the room is dark I can see in the light of the alarm clock's blue digital numbers, 12:32. I can see my hooves. I am too scared to move, too scared to turn around. The newspaper is lying on the floor. The brother in Minnesota is probably still at his security job after having worked all day at the chicken plant. I wonder if his sister is home asleep or if she is out at the bar with her college friends. It seems important to know. It seems important to understand whether or not it is worth it to sacrifice your life for someone else.

I feel the poke again. It is sharp. There's no mistaking it. I let my breath out, resigned. I get all four legs underneath me. They tremble as I turn, prepared for what I might deserve.

The digital clock changes to 12:33. There is no gun.

He has his front hoof raised. A buck, almost twice my size with nearly eight points of antlers, is waiting, his leg raised. The light of the clock reflects dully in the curve of his worn antlers. My front knees loosen and shake. I stumble. My head dips away from him. There is a deer in my bedroom, one besides me, and I am terrified, more terrified than I would be by all the guns in the world. I know what a gun means. I haven't any idea what a deer means.

I lift my eyes to him. He winces again when we meet. He lowers his hoof down to the rug and, turning his back on me, walks from the bedroom. It is then I pick up his scent. His mother gave birth to him. High school. A tire plant. Akron. Heavy machinery. The dinner I made him just hours ago. Mine.

I follow him out into our living room. "How?" I want to ask him, but we are both deer now and deer cannot speak. His neck is bent and he is maneuvering between his antlers, working on something. He has the front doorknob in his mouth, in his jaws. He twists his head, opening the door as if he's done this a hundred times before. The door sticks with the humidity but he shoves it open with his neck. He's really good at opening the door with his mouth, practiced. I feel the night rush in and he stands back from it, looking up at me. I can't be sure what he is saying. Either "Get out" or "Come on." His deer eyes are dark and hard to read. But he is waiting for me to do something. I nudge the screen door with my nose. I walk out in front of him, scared to leave because will he follow or simply lock the door behind me, kick me out?

The night is navy blue. Stars and cold. The grass underfoot breaks into a spicy smell, oregano and dirt. Why should anyone be afraid of night? But then there is motion around me like standing in a flooded river and I'm terrified. I am afraid of this night. I stumble back, trying to figure out what I'm looking at, to let the world come into focus. Fur and flanks and pointy hips and rib cages pass slowly before me. Sharp ears that nervously twitch forward and back. Everywhere the warmth of blood. Dark brown eyes lined with white fur and quivering backs that shake an itch. Silence. The road, the yard, the whole county is filled with deer, a calm stampede of them. An ocean of brown fur moving both together and separately, the way a caterpillar's back will resist and accept the ground at the same time. Some deer going up the road, some going down. They thread one another. Not one of the deer says a word. It's quiet. Each looks exactly the same, a flood of the ordinary. I am humiliated by their numbers, by the way they clump themselves together desperately like insects.

I turn to go back inside our house, but he is standing on the front step. He stomps his foot. He doesn't want us to go back in. He curls his spine and jumps, or not jumps but lurches quickly, urging me forward, as if that is where we both belong, as if that is where we've both always been. I know where forward is headed. I look out at the passing deer again, trying to pick out just one from the mass. This is hard to do. They are guarding what's individual by disguising it with what's not. See one leaf in a forest.

My husband steps forward in front of me. He is staring at the deer, the way a person might stare at the sea—without thought, without time. I catch a scent. What do the deer mean? That is a good question. That is the best question. I think the answer is somewhere nearby. I can smell it. I think I could almost say what the answer is but I am a deer now and deer can't talk.

My husband steps forward again and I follow him right up to the edge of the deer. His antlers have eight points. I tell myself I'll remember. I'll find him or hope he will find me, or maybe being found won't matter when we are animals. I step forward and then I step forward again, closer to the deer. I feel the warmth of that many living things. I feel their plainness rising up to swallow me. I step forward into the stream of beasts.

THE YELLOW

With his mother and father out of town for the weekend, Roy was left to forage for food in their nearly empty refrigerator. Was he physically or mentally unable to go grocery shopping? To order takeout from a restaurant? No, he wasn't.

Roy nibbled on a raw-onion-and-Cheddar sandwich. The rattling house unnerved him and the sandwich was too strong. It was an angry sandwich.

What made a house rattle? He couldn't say. He felt exposed in the kitchen. He abandoned his meal on the countertop and switched on the living room TV. He sat through the evening sitcoms, the late news, the late shows, and the start of a movie he'd not seen since 1985, telling himself that the noises he heard were wires scraping the siding in the wind. Even if they weren't.

At forty-two, he was living in his parents' house again, eating their food, driving their car from job interview to job interview.

"A pity," his grandmother had labeled him at a cook-out. They sat alone in weak folding chairs made weaker by the uneven ground. With no one else around to hear her declaration, she'd be able to deny it later. Or perhaps she thought he'd already gone inside. Macular degeneration. He'd walked away silently in case.

Near two in the morning, sick from so much TV, his grandmother's pronouncement in his head, Roy riled himself into a fury of self-improvement. He spent the early-morning hours in his bedroom tearing down homemade Bevis Frond posters and a paper chain he'd fashioned from gum wrappers. He moved all the furniture—except his bed and his dresser—up to the attic. In the basement, Roy found a half-full can of paint his father had used to mark the curb out front as a no-parking zone. Roy carefully began to paint his walls bright yellow.

He went without sleep. What was sleep to him? And by eleven the next morning his work was done. He sat cross-legged on the floor inhaling heady fumes. Yellow was everywhere. Yellow and calm. Fear and confusion had left. Possibility and sunshine became his friends. In the yellow, he felt himself the newborn child of Patti Smith and Jacques Cousteau. Roy rolled a cigarette and visualized foreign, gentler lands: India, Morocco, Florida.

Eventually, Sunday evening, his parents returned. His father, registering the new color of the walls, asked: "Son, did you turn faggot over the weekend?"

Roy offered no comeback. He held on to the color. He picked a flake of tobacco from his tongue and admired his father's use of the verb "turn." Turn was precisely what

Roy had done after three days of ripening in silence. He'd turned. He'd fermented into something wonderful and open, something porous and bright yellow.

Susanne's turning, on the other hand, had been far more subtle. Perhaps she didn't even realize she had turned, or maybe turning comes easier to women, acclimated as they are to miracles and pregnancies. Of which, by the age of thirty-nine, she'd had three.

Roy walked out on his father without answering. He grabbed the car keys from the kitchen table. He drove, and while he drove he tangled with the scan button on the car radio. "Don't Do Me Like That." "Don't Bring Me Down." "Love Is a Rose." "Straight Tequila Night." He liked all those songs, but that didn't stop him from continuing to seek. There had to be something more—his itchy finger was sure. And there was. "Blue Eyes Crying in the Rain." The song made him forget that his much younger sister would be getting married next month. He drove, open, porous, and yellow, his tires floating above the asphalt. He drove, threading together seams and streets, all his ideas, until, quite suddenly, the night became rigid. In one moment, there was nothing—no music, no thoughts, just a pure electric shock of adrenaline. Something black and furry had darted out into the road, frozen in Roy's headlights, and tumbled out of view. Squeals, brakes, and wrong-sounding mechanical thumpings followed. He had hit a dog. Roy had hit someone's dog.

Pulling off onto the soft shoulder, he felt a certain resistance from the undercarriage. The vehicle and the animal had been joined in a terrible union. He sat without moving. Perhaps it wasn't a dog. Perhaps it was some other creature, a beast unnamed and unknown, part woman, part deer. The thought gave him pause. He sat. Not long but long enough to know the thing was truly dead. There'd be no watching it limp away into the dark night, no gnashing teeth. He would not have to back the car up and over the creature. He would not have to kill it a second time.

Eventually Roy got out and the night stayed silent.

He circled the vehicle two, three times. There was nothing to be seen. Overhead, black branches cut their silhouettes on the navy sky. Roy crouched and there it was. Just a dog. Simple. Its body had been wedged behind a back wheel. Roy grabbed its tail and yanked the broken thing out from under. Something tore like fabric. The neck was soft and floppy like a harshly used work shirt. The dog was dead for certain. Roy hoisted the animal into his arms and set out for the nearest driveway. He could see it up ahead. An outdoor floodlight spilled onto the road in a narrow swath, most of the light getting trapped in the yard by a line of tall maples. The dog's body, not yet cold, warmed Roy and kept his arms from shaking.

Roy rang the bell, but Susanne was vacuuming. He carried the dog around to the side door. Front doors are for holidays. The dog's brown eye caught the light. It was no holiday. As Roy waited on the stoop, Susanne, with a vacuum hose in hand—her exhausted life—came into view. His knocking grew more desperate. He couldn't very well leave the carcass on her doorstep. He'd be forced to carry the dog from house to house until he found someone either heartbroken or intrepid enough to claim it.

She started when she saw Roy. It wasn't a busy street but the sort where too much wealth kept neighbors from dropping by unannounced.

Earlier, Susanne's husband had detected a certain ticking in her. He'd packed their children into the car for a night of pizza and a double feature at the second-run movie theater, leaving her alone to explode, to splatter the house with a combination of things she'd ingested as a teenager—films and punk rock records that confirmed what she'd guessed back then: one dies alone.

Best to have her family out of the way. Best to have them hidden in a dark cinema when the desire surged to chop her hair roughly and live on cigarettes. These bursts of freedom, while infrequent, were dangerous. Their self-indulgence could tear holes in evenings, marriages, families.

She'd been lost in the roar of the vacuum—a device that had the power to put her under a spell so she could contemplate the nature of the universe, the purpose of love, the purpose of death, and a fantasy she sometimes had of being bound nude to a parking meter in the city.

It was in this trancelike state that she saw Roy. What was he holding? She shut off her vacuum by yanking the plug from the wall. She opened the door.

"Hello."

"Hello."

"I'm afraid I've killed someone's dog."

"Yes," she confirmed. "That's Curtains. He belongs to my children."

"Curtains?"

"It's an old story." And then, looking at the animal again, "Oh, dear." She reached out and took the dog's body from Roy and, for one moment, like an uninspired actor in the uninspired film her husband and children were just then watching, she brushed the skin of Roy's forearm. She held his eyes, trying to remember if they'd met before.

"Poor Curtains."

They had never met.

"Oh," Roy said. "Oh, no. I'm so sorry." When nervous, he adopted an inflection that was not his own. His voice ratcheted up into a phony British accent, as if British accents were so appropriate, so authoritative that they could make any American dog be not dead. "I'm dreadfully sorry." There it was. London, England, done very poorly.

Roy hoped that maybe she'd wanted the dog dead for some reason. Maybe she'd grown tired of feeding him or accidentally petting those hard body lumps that old dogs get.

"I'm sorry." Roy tucked his chin in shame. "He came out of nowhere. I didn't even have a chance to brake. I'm sorry. Let me give you some money for a new dog." He reached for his wallet. He was broke. "What does a dog cost?" There was sixteen bucks in his wallet.

"Two hundred and fifty dollars," Susanne said. She carried the dog into the living room. "For a mutt."

"Oh." He fumbled and followed her. Two hundred and fifty seemed like robbery. "Can I write you a check?" He had two hundred and sixty-seven dollars in his bank account. If he wanted, he could go to an ATM tonight and withdraw it all, long before she could cash his check.

Susanne covered Curtains with an afghan that had been draped across the couch. She crouched in front of the dog, shielding him from Roy. What a thing for her dog to do— run out in front of a stranger's car and open himself up. What desperation. Curtains should have come to her, Susanne thought foolishly. Don't go to strangers, Curtains. There was blood on Roy's jacket. Blood on her arm, in her hair. Curtains's insides made pornographically public. Death really was mortifying. "A check is fine. Make it out to Susanne Martin."

"Susanne Martin. Certainly." He found a seat and began to write.

One surprisingly rigid paw stuck out from beneath the blanket. She knew the paw well, dipped in white fur, claws that alternated black, ivory, black, ivory. A piano on her dog's foot. She felt the dog lose his heat. She felt his body go cold.

As Susanne bent to hold his paw to her cheek, Roy saw that she loved the dog and he knew he wouldn't go to the ATM. He joined her on the floor, wrapping a stiff arm around her shoulders. He stowed the check away in his jacket pocket. "Sh-h-h. There, now. There, now."

Roy and Susanne sat by the rigid dog. She whimpered. She sounded like a tiny door creaking open. She wept and sniffled, wept and sniffled. Roy studied the wall's molding, the wall itself, a trace of dust along the molding's shaped ridge, an electrical outlet. What had he been thinking before the accident? He tapped his free hand against his temple and drew a blank.

Underneath his hand her shoulder felt cushioned in a way that his wasn't. There was her skin. There was her muscle. There was her bone, her blood, and all the blood's attendant particles keeping her alive, particles whose names he'd never know. They were strangers except for this dead dog. He thought of the yellow and turned toward Susanne, locating her lips with his own—some way of knowing her. Susanne did not react and, after a few slow moments with his mouth resting motionless on hers, he inserted a pointed tongue. She accepted it.

Roy and Susanne lay back on the rug beside the dog's carcass, beside the coffee table. Beneath the burned odor left by the vacuum, he could smell the dust still in the rug—salt and sand and dried skin from her kids, her husband, her now dead dog. Roy inhaled. And they stayed there locked in a silent trade. It wasn't a kiss, exactly, but something equally spectacular. The night, for all the species of insects alive in it, barely noticed.

Eventually, time passed and he buried his fingers in the hair at the nape of her neck. He pulled her closer. His other arm found the small of her back and used this handle to unlock some ancient pattern; their bodies began to move.

My dog died for this bit of living, Susanne thought. She did not consider her husband. She brokered no possible connection between her husband and lying on the floor with a stranger.

Roy's hands moved to unfasten, unhook, undress their bodies, conducting an urgent experiment. Her face was still damp from crying. In the shock of this unexpected coupling, he pinned her to the floor and she was a bird. He found his way inside and Susanne filled the room with sound, incantations that started with the routine "Oh, yes. God, yes," and morphed into the unfamiliar "Take it. Take it all," before winding up at the unnatural "Paint your landscape. Storm. Storm. Storm." Not sexy, just peculiar. Pleasure remained a far-off cousin to whatever exchange they were having.

At last, his muscles and eyes trembled. A transfer was completed and the charge between them dimmed. A film of sweat developed some guilt, some old wonder. Both Roy and Susanne began to chill. He didn't look at her. He was unsure what he'd got in the trade, though he knew it wasn't inconsequential. Good for him.

I should remove myself, he thought, and was about to when he felt something rough and warm, damp and thick. Curtains was licking the sweat from his scapula.

With a scream, both naked man and naked woman recoiled. He rolled, boot-camp style, a protected ball, into the shelter of the baby grand. From there he eyed the dog with dread. Susanne jumped to her feet and up onto the frantic couch.

Curtains had come back from the dead.

The dog raised his brow, wondering why these humans should act so foolishly.

Susanne lifted her hands in surrender. "The dog was dead."

"The dog was dead," Roy confirmed. And it was true. They'd seen it and felt it. The dog, moments ago, had been ruined, limp, no more.

"How, Suse?" Their physical intimacy had shaved away the Anne. He cradled and rocked himself, a squatting troll: a head, a rounded back, and two feet sticking out from his torso. He looked grotesque underneath the piano.

Curtains licked the thin, pale fur between his legs.

"My dog is alive."

"But why? Why is your dog alive?"

Susanne scratched her left buttock. "You must have only knocked Curtains unconscious."

Roy looked from the dog to Susanne. "Then how come you don't want to touch him either?"

"Nonsense," Susanne said, readjusting her position of retreat. "Come here, boy. Here, Curtains."

The dog looked up from his lick and made his way over to the waiting hand. Susanne held her arm as far out from her body as possible. Curtains rubbed against it and Susanne immediately snapped her hand to her chest as if burned. She covered herself with a fleece blanket. "Back," she told the confused dog. "Back." Curtains, as dumb and happy as any non-dead dog, cocked his head and studied the hunkering humans before meandering into the kitchen to see if, in the time he'd been dead, someone had refilled his dish with kibble.

Quickly, Roy crawled out from underneath the piano. "What should we do?"

Susanne nodded. She stood, distancing herself from him. They were not a we. She dressed swiftly. Nodding,

nodding, nodding. She tightened a belt around her sweater. "So," she said, looking into the kitchen where Curtains had gone. "You'll have to kill it. Again."

Roy drew his eyes wide and wider. "What? It?"

"We've opened some sort of door here." She knelt in front of Roy, resting her hands on his knees as if they really were lovers. "It can't stay open. I have a good life." She pinched the meat of Roy's thighs. "You have to kill the dog."

He closed his eyes. Reasons and excuses assembled themselves. He was dealing with an unhinged person. He'd stumbled into a TV show. The dog had simply been knocked out.

Roy opened his eyes. "It won't work. That's like stuffing a baby back inside its mother. You think I'll just forget? I won't forget."

"Yes," Susanne said. "You will forget."

Once, as a girl, Susanne, alone in her grandmother's empty barn, had heard a voice speaking to her. The voice had said, "Bow at the river," or, maybe, "Cows at the river." It didn't matter what the voice had said, because Susanne, terrorized and unwilling to confront the unexplainable, the supernatural, had suppressed any memory of it. "You'll forget."

He put his head in his hands.

"You'll find some way to explain it. You'll call me a witch or a crazy person. Turn it into a dream. You'll forget." She stood and, searching Roy's coat, found the check, folded it, and put it in her pocket. "You have to kill him and then you have to leave."

Roy pulled his fingers through his hair, like a child having a tantrum. "But I don't believe in magic." He barely believed in God. He barely believed in chiropractors.

She kept her voice calm. "That's like not believing in car accidents. Just because you don't want them to happen doesn't mean they don't." She clucked at him, scolding. "It's not belief. It's whether or not you're going to let magic ruin your life. People pretend the world is ordinary every day." She held her hips. "Because they have to."

"Why don't *you* kill him?"

"Come on," she tsk-tsked. "You started this. You kissed me."

"It wasn't really a kiss," Roy said. All he'd done was paint his walls yellow. "And I definitely didn't raise your dog from the dead."

"Yeah?" She was leaving the room with sarcasm, matter settled. "Then what did?"

"I don't know," he told her, but Susanne, having plugged the vacuum back in, was no longer listening.

From the dark behind her house, he saw the warm glow of her windows, her family returning. He leaned on the shovel.

"Out! Out!" she had said. Once for Roy, once for Curtains. "There's a shovel in the shed."

Roy stood in the night undetected, looking in. Her children and her husband gathered around her, relaying the very thin but fantastically absurd plots of the Hollywood movies they'd seen. A bank heist and a clean getaway. A love that conquers all. A dog that comes back to life. Her young son's hands shook, his feet stomped, recalling the wonders. How true they'd been. Her daughter's head spun. Each world had been real enough to betray her by ending neatly after an hour and a half.

Susanne retracted the vacuum's cord. Tethered again. And in the dark Roy understood her family's pact. Work and school, laundry, dinner, the things that happened in their lives were not part of the brightness that she and Roy had glimpsed. These things had nothing to do with birth and death but were, rather, dull, quite expected, and entirely unastonishing. Nothing strange ever really happened. No, it didn't.

The weight of the shovel made Roy's arms burn. He needed to sit down. He needed to get back in his car, start the engine, drive away from here with his finger on the radio's scan button, looking for the right song, one that might erase Susanne, the dog, and the shovel she'd wanted him to use to brain and bury Curtains in her backyard.

The dog looked up at him, tilting its head a bit to one side, waiting for the blow of the shovel's blade. "No," Roy told him.

He would leave soon. He'd drive through the night listening as each song began, hot with promise. "I Feel for You." "Don't Stop Believin'." "Time After Time." Fine songs. He knew them well. He'd heard them all hundreds of times, as if he'd been driving the earth forever, killing any and all things that got in the way. None of the songs would ever make him forget and he told Curtains so. "Scram," he yelled. "Get out of here!"

Curtains turned and wandered off to pee on some rhododendrons, not at all like an animal running for its life.

The dog would be waiting on her doorstep tomorrow morning, gentle, stupid, still undead, still looking for something to eat. In front of her children she'd pretend to forget. She'd hold out her hand to pet the dog's head, and in a while, perhaps a few days or a week, the head would begin to feel like the head of any dog. By the light of day, under the huge yellow, optimistic sun, Susanne would find it easy to convince herself of anything: marriage is easy, motherhood a snap, and death uncomplicated. But in the dark it was clear to Roy. Susanne sat on the couch, surrounded by her family, while out in the night, partner to the extraordinary, Roy held a shovel made for digging deeper in the dirt.

CORTÉS THE KILLER

It's starting to get dark. Beatrice walks the highway's shoulder from the bus depot to her family's house. She stays just outside the guardrail on the dry grass strewn with trash, matted down by road salt and rain. There's the bloated body of a dead raccoon. Beatrice is sure that every car and truck passing holds someone she knew in high school. Inside their cars they ask, "Is that Beatrice? What is she doing with a raccoon carcass?"

She turns up the drive. She hasn't seen the farm in more than a year. After her father died she moved away to the city—not for any good reason, but now she likes it there because the humiliations of entering her thirties as a single woman happen behind a closed apartment door, out of the view of her family and everyone she's ever known.

There are some weathered plastic Easter decorations wired to the front porch, a hip-high bunny rabbit and a bright green egg purchased at the drugstore. It is

Thanksgiving. In the time she's been gone redneck clones of her brother and her mother have had their perverted redneck way with the house.

The farm is an island in a sea of big chain stores. While the surrounding farms were plowed under one by one and turned into shopping centers, her parents had stood by. They had waited rather than selling as the neighbors all had. They had waited with the thought, *Maybe this will stop, maybe the farms will return.* Now, along a ten-mile strip of parking lots, stores, gas stations, banks, and supermarkets, their farm is the only one left.

It isn't even much of a farm. Beatrice's parents gave up farming seven years before when, one morning, Beatrice's mother told her father, "I don't feel like getting out of bed." He looked her over and, holding her jaw in his hands, he studied her face for a long while before saying, "Yeah. I can see it. Right there on your forehead," as if there were a word written across her brow that excused her from farm-work for the rest of her life.

Within a few weeks Beatrice's father had become an expert crossword puzzle solver. He'd even considered writing a novel before realizing that soon they would be broke. Beatrice's parents had to start working or sell the farm. So they leased their land out to a conglomerate soybean operation and applied for jobs in the new industrial park. Her father found work as a loan adjuster, her mother a job in advertising, working in the satellite office of a company called Mythologic Development, where they turn myths and sometimes history into marketable packages used for making new products and ideas more digestible to the consumer public. Her father didn't like having an office job. He used his sick days as soon as he got them, but Beatrice's mother had always been very dramatic, someone who would swoon or leap without provocation; the sort of person who would sing while grocery shopping and then wonder why people were staring at her. She flourished during the brainstorming conference calls that were a regular feature of her new job. She'd dominate the conversations with her patched-together notions of Leda and the Swan, the void of Ginnungagap, the bubonic plague, and Hathor the Egyptian goddess, whom she reenvisioned as a nineteen-year-old Ukrainian supermodel spokesperson for a vodka company.

Beatrice's parents hadn't been born farmers. It was just one of many bright ideas they'd developed in their twenties, ideas like dropping out of college in their junior year, forgoing regular dentist visits, and having children they decided to name Beatrice and Clement.

"Right," Clem says after Thanksgiving dinner, standing to leave the table. He shakes his head at his mother, at Beatrice. Clem works as a carpenter, though he's mostly interested in small projects, cabinets and decks, hand-carving the names of rock bands into soft pieces of wood.

"Going to toke up?" Beatrice's mother asks him. He pops his head back inside the kitchen. He is stocky and solid like a bolted zucchini that has grown too long. He holds a finger and thumb up to his lips and inhales, pinching together a vacancy in between them.

Their mother has put a feather in her hair for the holiday, her "Indian headdress." She can't stand it that her youngest child is a pothead and sometimes she'll get a look, as if she's trying not to cry just thinking about it. She's a very good actress. She stares at Clem. He looks just like her, dark hair, red skin, and papery lips. Beatrice's mother can make her bottom jaw tremble so slightly that the movement is barely perceptible. She stares at him with her mouth wide open, waiting for him to feel guilty. Beatrice looks away. It is difficult for Beatrice to think of her mother as someone with thoughts and desires, as someone who keeps a vibrator in her bedside drawer the way Beatrice does, as someone who might dream about a tremendous ice cube, the size of a sofa, melting in the middle of a hot desert, and wake up having absolutely no idea what the dream means.

"Dude, I'm so stoned." Clem laughs once, faking a stumble before disappearing. As he opens the front door the flat sound of road traffic sneaks inside. Beatrice clears the table. She holds the turkey over the garbage by its breastbone, dangling it there while her mother splits what is left in the last wine bottle between their two glasses.

"When Atlantis was sinking there was an awful period of . . ." and Beatrice's mother stops to think of the proper word but can't. "Of sinking," she says and places her open hands on either side of her face, like the sunshine. Beatrice cringes at the gesture. Her mother is going to try to tell her something she doesn't want to hear. Her mother still works for Mythologic and believes all concepts are better communicated through specious retellings of ancient myths. Most of the time, Beatrice can't see the connections.

"Imagine," her mother says, her hands still in place. "People went to sleep inland and woke up with the ocean at their doors. When they stepped outside in the morning to pee or to feed their goats the neighbors were gone and the only sound was waves lapping."

Her mother slowly drags one finger across their kitchen table and then does it again. Beatrice remains entirely still, frozen like a field rabbit, hoping her mother will decide not to tell her whatever it is she wants to say. She can already imagine its perimeters: "Honey, I wish you would think about a job that offers insurance," or "I know a real nice young man you might like to meet, Bea." But he wouldn't be a nice young man. He would be another forty-five-year-old divorced actor her mother had met through community theater projects, a man who also holds his hands up around either side of his face like the sunshine when he wants to make a point.

Or maybe she wants to tell Beatrice that she is finally going to sell the farm.

But Beatrice is wrong.

"When your dad was in the hospital the doctor gave me a choice, Bea." She rubs her palms across her skinny thighs, exhaling. "The doctor asked, 'Do you want to stop his pain?' And at first I said, yeah, of course, but then the doctor asked again, 'No. Do you really, really want to stop his pain?' And, Bea, I knew what he meant and I said yes. I killed your dad."

She is drunk.

"Oh. So *you* killed him?"

"Well, not me, but the doctor. I told the doctor to go ahead and get it over with."

"What does that have to do with Atlantis?" Beatrice asks.

Her mother has to think for a moment. She looks up at the ceiling. "We all have to die sometime?"

Beatrice stares straight ahead like a TV stuck on static, the remote control gone dead. She blinks a series of gray and black squiggled lines. No reception. Nothing. Her mother's words are not getting through; they are stones dropped into a bottomless hole, the hollow known as Beatrice. They fall and fall until they are too far away to be heard.

There's an unwound egg timer beside the stove. "You want to watch a movie, hon?" Static clears, program resumes. It's a story about a mother and her kids on a farm in Pennsylvania, a dull after-school special broadcast for the Thanksgiving holiday.

If Beatrice sits in the living room with her mother watching a movie, she'll explode—a dark green syrup of boredom her mother will have to sponge off the floor with Fantastik and a towel. "I'm going to go see what Clem's up to." Beatrice is still holding the turkey by its breastbone. It has started to sway. Beatrice drops the bird. It makes a swoosh, a rush of flight as it falls into the garbage bag.

When Beatrice was a girl, Clement still a baby, and the farm was in okay shape, Bea and her father walked the fields once a day. The furrows were dry and bulging and Beatrice liked how it felt when the dirt broke underneath her muck boots. Corn plants made a canopy over her head. She'd lose sight of everything except her father's legs marching ahead of her. She'd put her hand inside his and he'd hold it roughly as if her hand was a mouse he'd captured. She'd pretend he was not her father at all but a boyfriend, someone from TV.

He said: "Don't tell your mom, but I'm the king of the farmers." They walked on a bit farther and came across an irrigation hose that had cracked its rubber tubing. Her father fingered the leak and stared out at the land with every intention of coming back and patching up the cracked hose. He'd never come back. He just liked to look that way from time to time.

"Farming," he'd say, "takes ten percent perspiration and ninety percent inspiration." Beatrice had heard this the other way around, but didn't let on. Maybe he was the king. He wasn't a bad farmer. He just didn't do things the way they had always been done. For instance, pruning trees— he had no time for it, or thinning plants. He hated to yank up seedlings that had been eager enough to sprout. He'd let the vegetables grow on top of one another. He'd let the carrots and beets twist around each other, deformed by proximity. "They still taste as sweet," he'd say, but no one wanted to buy the bent oddities that came from such close growing quarters.

Beatrice's father rarely wore proper farmer clothing. Instead he dressed in chinos, button-down oxford shirts, and canvas sneakers. "They're cheap" is all he ever had to say. He looked like James Dean in the movie *East of Eden*. James Dean on a John Deere. He'd hay the fields, and Beatrice would follow behind in the trail of the tractor's exhaust, so it would be hard for her to know what was an act and what was real.

Sodium vapor lamps from the mall parking lots wash away any definition for miles around. Everything on the farm glows the same yellow gray at night. Beatrice trips on a pig trough her mother's been using as a planter for impatiens.

"What's up, dude?" her brother asks when she yelps. Clem has converted half of the barn into an apartment. She stumbles in. There are no locks on his apartment because his door is an old cellar hatch taken off a house demolished to make way for a Dunkin' Donuts. His kitchen countertops are built from plywood the Home Depot used as concrete molds and then tossed. Most of his apartment is built from stuff he lifted off construction sites. It's a common practice among Clem's friends because they can't yet not own the land they've always owned. "Matthew Campbell's milking pavilion used to be here, so I guess we can just help ourselves."

"Let's go downtown," Beatrice says. "See if the stores are open on Thanksgiving."

"I guess." Clem's uncertain about going out in the cold, but still enough under the sway of his older sister that he'll do what she wants to do. He detaches himself from his video game.

"Can I try that first?" she asks.

"This?" He holds the controller up. "Yeah, yeah sure." He restarts the game. "Do you know how to play?"

"No."

"I'll start you off slowly." He slips her hand into a glove that is rigged with controls. It is filled with tiny nodes like suction cups, the dead raccoon's puckered skin. "Sit down," he says, and she does.

At first nothing happens. The screen turns blue and the nodes tickle her hand. Clem fusses with the machinery.

The apartment is tiny and the walls are mostly covered with shelves and cabinets. Clem moved out of the main house when he fell in love with Anna. They moved into the barn together after high school and lived here for almost five years. But Anna moved away to the city a year ago. She hasn't picked up all her stuff yet. Clothes, some textbooks that she and Clem kept from school, and a nice set of silver that Anna's grandparents gave her. Everything is covered with bits of old hay from the barn. Sometimes Anna and Beatrice meet up for coffee in the city. They never talk about the farm or Clem. They act like survivors from a low-budget, straight-to-DVD apocalypse.

The video game starts up. A woman walks through a Zen Buddhist garden, wearing a tight silver outfit, carrying a long sword.

"That's you. Use the glove to go forward."

Beatrice walks slowly through the garden, because someone is going to tiptoe up behind her with a horrible machete, and she's had a number of glasses of red wine. She's not sure she can fight back. Beatrice feels the girl walk, inside the girl's digital skin.

Clem lights a joint and hums the video game's theme, a soundtrack. The girl on the screen creeps forward, flashes the blade of her sword. Beatrice accepts the joint with her ungloved hand, jerking the controls. The girl on-screen stands still, doing nothing, flicking her sword, walks backward, looks toward the couch. Beatrice holds the smoke in her lungs long enough for both of them.

There are pathways to the left and the right in the garden. Beatrice can't turn yet. Clem hums the tune. Beatrice exhales, imagining a man with a deep radio voice speaking over the music, whispering into Beatrice's ear, reading her the fine print. It fills her with longing just the same.

A pack of ninja warriors surprises her from above, and after a very short fight Beatrice is dead.

It is colder than most Thanksgivings. The ruts in the driveway have solidified, forming seals of creaky ice. Beatrice and Clem walk to his truck in silence. She still feels as if she's on-screen with the video game's sharpened abilities. She controls the world with her hand, senses sounds with her skin, hears her brother's fingers jangle the keys in his pocket. She hears her mother sigh as the mid-movie commercial break starts. Beatrice hasn't smoked pot in a long time. She feels every person who has ever stepped on the driveway. Oil deliverymen. Tractor repairmen. Lenape Indians. She feels the outline of these people precisely, solid bodies beneath her feet. She squishes faces with her boots.

Beatrice has an idea. "Let's take Humbletonian," she says, letting go of the truck's door handle. Humbletonian is a horse. When her parents sold the farm animals they kept a few chickens for eggs and one horse named Humbletonian. Her father named the horse this because she was not a Hambletonian. A Hambletonian is a very distinguished trotting horse. A Humbletonian is nothing. It is like changing your name to Stonerfeller because you are not a Rockefeller.

"In the trailer?" her brother asks, and then answers the question himself. "No. Ride the horse into town? Right? Right. Cool," he says, eyes glassy. They walk back to the barn, breaking ice again.

After their father stopped farming he sometimes took a sleeping bag to the loft above the horse's stable after dinner. He'd smoke cigarettes up there and spend the night like a Boy Scout. He thought that the horse's wild nature could make him feel better about working in an office. He thought the horse could soothe the unease in his rib cage. From the loft her father pretended he was Jerry Lee Lewis, an old table saw platform for the piano. He'd sing to the horse. "You. Leave. Me." Pause. Pause. "Breathless." Though her father's odd behavior seemed exciting at the time, Beatrice now thinks that horses aren't wild. Horses can't soothe our unease in the world. Horses are about the most broken, unwild creatures in existence, except for maybe burros and dogs. They do exactly what humans tell them to do. So when she thinks now how her father slept in the barn, rode Humbletonian across their forty acres because he thought it would cure the unease in his chest, it only makes her sad. That wasn't unease, Dad. It was lung cancer.

"Hello, pumpkin pie." Clem pets Humbletonian's nose. The barn smells yellow—urine and old pine boards.

The horse's belly sags in a way that reminds Beatrice of a velour reclining chair. "Hello, La-Z-Boy girl." Beatrice kisses the horse. Humbletonian does not look particularly happy to see her. Clem attaches bit and bridle. He puts a hand on the saddle straddling the stable wall, but Beatrice shakes her head no. Clem leads the horse outside by the reins and crouches down on one knee, keeping the other lifted square. Beatrice uses Clem's knee as a boost and climbs up onto the horse's bare back. "Whoop," Beatrice whoops. In a moment her brother is seated behind her. Clem wraps big zucchini arms around her sides, reaching for the reins.

Brother and sister are quiet as they trot through harvested fields. The sound of dead stalks and frost crunching under Humbletonian's hooves fills the gray quiet of the night. The video game's theme song rattles in the back of Beatrice's head.

"I don't know what she'll think of the road," Clem says. "I don't think she's ever been past the far field." Their mother only uses the horse when her car gets stuck in the muddy divots of their driveway. She harnesses Humbletonian to the bumper, pulling while she pushes.

They reach the end of the driveway. Humbletonian turns left and trots along the breakdown lane, as if she can't wait to get down to town, as if there's nothing to it.

On the road Humbletonian's hooves sound like winter—metal on ice or an empty galvanized pail tossed down a stone staircase. They pass an abandoned barn that is wedged between two service stations and two narrow swaths of dried red clover. Someone has spray-painted the words LUV SHAK below a tin sign advertising the Crystal Cave tourist attraction. The land is flat and open here. The road is the straightest road there is. It runs all the way down to where the Pennsylvania Dutch people live in villages named Blue Ball, Intercourse, Paradise.

An eighteen-wheeled tanker whooshes past Humbletonian. It blows Beatrice's body to the right. A car honks before passing. The man in the backseat does not seem surprised to see a horse and riders on the highway on Thanksgiving evening. He throws his cigarette butt toward them so it explodes against the asphalt, a bomb sized for insects.

"I'm going to puke," she says.

"No. No, you won't." Clem pats her on the back one, two, three times. Beatrice leans against Humbletonian's neck. The warmth of the horse on her stomach. They ride the rest of the way in silence except for the click of Humbletonian's hooves and the rush of the horse's warm pulse.

One of the myths Beatrice's mother was responsible for developing was a fictionalized version of Montezuma meeting Cortés for the first time. Her mother's coworkers rarely bothered to differentiate between those things that had actually happened and those things that people just used to say had happened. They'd take history and add to it and no one knew the difference anymore. For example, they might say that Montezuma could fly through the air carrying three virgins at a time to a sacrificial altar in the sky. They might say that there was bloodshed when these two men met or that Cortés was part man, part horse.

Mythologic Development sold the Montezuma-Cortés myth to an amusement park in Maryland, which used it for a roller coaster called the Aztecathon. The concept sold for a good price, but her mother was a salaried employee and so she saw very little of the money. Now the amusement park owns Montezuma. He is their intellectual property.

Beatrice's mother keeps a painting of Montezuma over her bed. In the painting he looks more like a famous movie star than like an Aztec ruler. Beatrice's mother likes that about him. She tells Beatrice that she is in love with Montezuma now that Beatrice's father is gone.

"Montezuma's also dead," Beatrice says, and her mother smiles as if that were a really good joke.

"Who-ah." Humbletonian turns into the Middleland Mall Complex. They pass through a large empty lot dotted with circles of light. It is freezing cold. "Who-ah." Humbletonian clops to a halt outside the Walmart entrance. At the doors, they wait on the horse. Their breath is visible in the cold air. Humbletonian stomps her hoof as though asking, "What next?" Her motion is detected by a sensor. The door swings open to let them in. Humbletonian takes a few steps back before she steadies.

They'd have to duck their heads to make it through the entry. "I bet they've never had a horse inside there." Clem tilts his neck. A security officer stationed by the theft-deterrent column stands to adjust his utility belt. He eyes their transportation with more than suspicion. He steps outside.

"I know you're not even thinking about bringing that beast in here," he says.

"But I *was* thinking of it," Clem says. "So you're wrong."

The guard palms his nightstick. He looks like just the

sort of security officer who would have Clem ticketed for an inane livestock violation still on the books from 1823. No Horse-Riding on Public Holidays. Clem slides off Humbletonian, leading Beatrice over to the corral for collecting shopping carts. He ties Humbletonian's reins to the metal bar. Beatrice slides off the curve of her flank.

Few people seem to be shopping. Clem asks a young man in a Walmart smock, "Excuse me. What's going on here?"

The young man raises his eyebrows, waiting for some clue as to how he can assist them. "Lots of things are going on here," the boy says finally.

"Walmart's open?" Clem asks. "It's Thanksgiving."

The boy stares at the dog food he's been pricing, looking to the back of the shelf, seeing something golden but invisible to everyone else.

Clem bends to see what the boy's looking at. Just the back of the metal shelf. Clem grabs Beatrice's arm and leads her away.

Up front, the store is ready for Christmas. Past Christmas comes an aisle of automotive and craft/hobby supplies, then an aisle of hair products and footwear, then an aisle of watches and diamond-chip rings. All of these aisles dead-end at the wall of sporting goods/hunting gear. Ladies' and menswear are intersected by a row of birthday cards, logic-puzzle books, scented candles, deodorant, and toothpaste. Beatrice and Clem pass the electronics division. They're sold out of the game Clem was thinking about buying, Dead or Alive 5000. There is a paper SALE sign that Clem swipes at.

"Do you need anything?"

Beatrice detects a flashing pulse in the fluorescent lighting. "Nope. Let's go."

Clem takes a pack of gum, puts it in his pocket. "For Mom," and they leave quickly without paying for the gum.

Outside, Humbletonian is no longer tied up. She is gone, and Beatrice bets it was the security guard. "Shit." Clem giggles because, by the shopping-cart corral, there is a pile of horseshit that Humbletonian left behind.

Clem scans the parking lot. The circles of light underneath each lamp are still there, but no horse. "You go that way," Clem tells Beatrice. "I'll go this way and I'll meet you around back. We'll flush her out." Clem departs around one side of the giant complex and Beatrice walks off in the other direction.

The store is so long that she feels as though she'll never even reach the corner of it. Beatrice is an astronaut dragging a two-hundred-pound space suit. That's why her footsteps can't carry her forward. She stops altogether. "I wouldn't have killed him," Beatrice says out loud. She waits until she hears a question from the far side of her brain, from her mother. "What would you have done? Just let him suffer? Let him go on breathing that bubbly wet breath that sounded like a damn water fountain?" "Yes," Beatrice answers. "Yes, I would have."

The Walmart does not end. It goes on and on, windowless and solid. Beatrice thinks of the old cartoons. An illustrator draws two panels of background, a desert or a pine forest, and by bringing one panel in front of the other, he can keep it going forever, a duplicated landscape Wile E.

Coyote can run through. If she had four legs like Humbletonian she'd be able to get around the back of the mall faster. She thinks to skip but after ten or eleven lengths her lungs chug and backfire on the cold air. She walks the rest of the way.

Behind the shopping center there are bulldozers, at least twenty of them huddled with their backs to Beatrice, in a private conference. It's freezing. Apart from the dozers there's nothing here except a gigantic hole. It is tremendous, far larger than a football field, and it is filled with water. In the dark, the hole extends beyond the limit of Beatrice's vision. Clem is already standing at the edge, looking down into it. Humbletonian is there, too. She has climbed down into the pit and is walking across the surface of the ice formed there. It's like a lake. Maybe one of the bulldozers broke a water pipe while digging. There's a lot of water here, a reservoir's worth, or, Beatrice hopes not, frozen sewage. Humbletonian is walking across the ice, bending every now and again to lick the surface.

"Woo-hoo! Humbletonian!" Clem yells. "Good horse. Good horse," he shouts. Humbletonian turns from where she is, halfway across the ice, and when she sees Clem and Beatrice she begins to trot across the very center of the pit toward them, more like a dog than a horse. Her coat is as silver as the ice, and beautiful.

Beatrice lifts up her arms and shakes her hips. "Woo-hoo! Horsey!" she calls. Time slows to a pace where Beatrice can notice every single thing. Humbletonian's muscles, her breath coming out of her flared nostrils, and the odd rhythm of her trot. She notices the gorgeous ice and dirt and the lovely darkness, thick as felt, existing in this ugly place. She can hear each hoof as it falls against the ice. Beauty stands nearby, a shadowy person whose exhales become Beatrice's inhales, warming her up. This moment of warmth, this beautiful horse. A jealous hole cracks open in the ice, swallowing the back legs and hindquarters of Humbletonian faster than thought.

Humbletonian tries to clear the water, but each clop of her front hooves shatters what she's grabbed. There can't be that much water underneath her. But she's not touching the bottom. Clem starts to swear, but slowly; everything is happening so slowly at first that time will come to a halt and the world behind the shopping center will be all right. It might even be possible to ignore the drowning horse. Beatrice and her brother are here only in a dream. They will both wake up soon.

Beatrice reaches her arms even higher. "Clem," she says. Clem wrings his hands. He lowers himself into the pit, down to where the ice starts. He is moving carefully. Humbletonian is thrashing. It's the only sound. The water must be freezing. "Clem," Beatrice says again, and again Clem wrings his hands so hard he might tear them off by his wrists. He steps out onto the edge of the ice and creeps toward Humbletonian. She is in up to her middle. Only her front hooves and her head are above the ice. Clem stops. The horse is twisting and snorting. She screams as much as a horse can scream. Clem raises his hands to his face. He takes another step toward the horse. "Clem," Beatrice repeats his name a third time. He turns to look at her. A seam has been cut open in Clem through the center of his face. A seam that says there is no way to stop this. No way for a man to save a horse drowning in freezing water. Clem brings his hands up to his ears and, pressing the small knobs of cartilage there, he stops listening.

Quiet moments pass. The static returns, as though it were being broadcast from nearby. Humbletonian starts giving up. The water has dropped her into shock. Beatrice can see a lot of white in the horse's eye, as though it had been pried open. It blinks dry air once more. Humbletonian's head goes under. Her forelegs, above the barrier of the ice, kick, emptying what's inside them. It is a gruesome convulsion.

"She's getting away." Beatrice skids on her heels down to where her brother stands. She walks out onto the ice. A loud crack bellows from the frozen water, like a whip pushing Beatrice back, away from her horse. Beatrice drops to her knees and Humbletonian goes under all the way. Their horse is gone. The water flattens out over her head.

Clem lowers his hands. "Don't." But Beatrice doesn't listen. She sits down on the ice and watches the hole where Humbletonian went. She slides toward it on her knees. The hole doesn't do anything.

The silence fills in around Beatrice and Clem like insulation. The two of them look down into the black hole, waiting, maybe, for some triumphant geyser, a phoenix, or Pegasus to rise up out of the water. Fifteen minutes pass, maybe half an hour before they recognize what they are staring at: an empty black hole.

"Clem." Beatrice has her back to him. "You know what Mom told me?"

"What?"

"She gave the doctor permission to kill Dad."

"Yeah, I know," Clem says.

"You know?"

"She asked me what I thought before she did it."

No one asked Beatrice. She sat by her father's hospital bed for days, rubbing lotion into the dry skin of his calves and feet, and no one said anything to her. "No one asked me."

"We already knew what you'd say."

Since her father's death, Beatrice's parents have been two-dimensional pieces of paper she folds up, tucks into her back pocket, and forgets about when she does her laundry, fishing them out of the lint trap later: her mother all things bad, her father all things good. But Clem ruins it every time. There's Clem, sitting on the ice, shaking his head, saying, "It's no one's fault, Bea." But Beatrice would like to find someone to blame.

Even with the static, she sees a map in front of her, a map of yesterday, today, and tomorrow. She sees that they arrived here at this future rather than a different one. One with horses. Maybe that future would have been better. But they had arrived here to a time when their farm is dead, when Beatrice has moved away to the city, when Clem is stuck in place, and when, most nights, her mother walks down to the end of the driveway, out to meet the incoming tide in Pennsylvania.

Beatrice leans forward, lowering her whole body onto the ice. She pushes herself on her stomach out to where the horse disappeared. She rests her cheek there for a long time. She pets her horse through the ice. "Don't go any farther," Clem says. Beatrice dips her hand inside the hole, into a land that is already lost.

THE HOUSE BEGAN
TO PITCH

She'd come for plywood as the radio advised. "Ma'am, can you swipe your card again?" Mysterious forces had erased the magnetic strip on her Visa. A manager is called over. Ada keels onto one hip while the people in line behind her rot and glare, their arms loaded with jugs of water, rolls of plastic. The air-conditioning raises gooseflesh on Ada's arms. She waits for the manager's approval.

It isn't until she wheels her purchases out to her car that the geometry of the situation strikes her. Her small sedan is no place for four sheets of plywood. Sweat makes dark circles on her tank top. She looks at the wood. She looks at her car. She tightens her ponytail, and rather than asking someone for help or going to get a refund, she drags her teeth across her top lip.

In a few hours this parking lot will steam as the first raindrops strike. The light fixtures will ping as the wind picks up. The orange *H* in the Home Depot sign might loosen from its moorings, taking flight across the state of Florida, a glorious end to a bright career.

She's done what they asked. She's bought plywood. She's just not going to take it home with her. Ada leaves the wood nosed into the island between car grilles, an offering. She starts her engine and Neil Young sings, "I saw your brown eyes turning once to fire." Signaling a right turn with her left hand crooked at the elbow, Ada pulls out of the parking lot.

When she moved here from Rhode Island, it took her three days to make the drive. She stopped at the halfway point to tell someone where she was headed. "Florida." She smiled.

The Virginia rest area worker, positioned behind the Visitor's Information desk, sneered. "Florida's an old coral reef. Geologically it's brand-new." He passed her a brochure for Colonial Williamsburg.

Brand-new and improved. Ada left the brochure behind.

When Ada arrived she bought a tiny one-story rectangle. A square house from the seventies with tall glass windows floor to ceiling, dark wood, and the occasional odor of mold that comes with basement-free homes. The neighborhood is nothing much, some mobile houses and a family who races ATVs down the street. But Ada eats breakfast on the lanai. She sleeps with the windows open, the sound of dry vegetation brushing against the stucco. Kingbirds spear bugs and dead flowers in her yard. Lizards inflate their pink necks. It is nothing like the version of Florida Rhode Island believes. That Florida is confined to tabloid headlines: 26-FOOT PYTHON FOUND UNDER-NEATH 75-YEAR-OLD WOMAN'S HOME or ALLIGATORS ON THE LOOSE IN SUBURBAN MIAMI.

Her neighbor Chuck is sitting half in, half out of his metal utility storage shed. It's lightweight, aluminum and fiberglass; the whole thing held together with wing nuts. Chuck has set a metal folding chair and a TV tray just outside the door. His sister, Patricia, has a three-bedroom home on the same property, but Chuck lives in his storage shed with no windows, no floor, and no plumbing. "I'm a green anarchist," he told Ada when they first met. The ideology has to do with caveman times, dumpster diving, and friends in prison for blowing up car dealerships. Chuck doesn't go shopping or burn fossil fuels. He rides a ten-speed bike in T-shirts magic-markered to read, RECLAIM! REWILD! RESIST! or STATE MELTDOWN or simply BURN, BURN, BURN.

His radio is tuned to the same station Ada's listening to in the car so that the broadcast comes through in stereo with a slight delay. "I repeat, SEVERE HURRICANE WARNING issued for southern Florida. We've got Chief John DeLamian here. Chief, what can you tell us?"

"Well, at this point, Mike, I can tell you we've got a SEVERE HURRICANE WARNING issued for southern Florida."

"Chief, maybe you could clarify for our listeners the difference between a WATCH and a WARNING."

"Sure thing, Mike. A WATCH means we're just watching, just gonna wait and see, while a WARNING—" Ada turns the car off.

"Hey, Chuck." She passes through the low row of palms dividing her land from Patricia's. Ada holds a two-fingers wave, an Indian chief coming in peace. "I couldn't get any plywood," she tells him.

"They sell out?"

"My car's too small."

"Ah ha," he says. "Well then, you're in for it. Total destruction."

"I guess so." She chews her lip again.

Chuck looks at her lopsided. She slept with him once, right after she'd moved here. In the intervening months she's not made that mistake again. "There's not much you can do to stop it, Ada. A hurricane will just take your ply-wooded house and deposit it upside down across the street."

"Those scenes on the news up north always looked faked. Like a Christmas village, trailers in trees."

"You must be some sort of monster." Chuck shakes his head. "Beer, monster?"

Nowhere does a storm appear yet. "Sure. Thank you."

He fishes her a can of malt liquor from out of an ice cooler. "Malt liquor gets the job done," he told her when they first met, and in the time she's known him she's found that to be true.

Dull sunlight shines into his shed. At the foot of his cot there's a small steamer trunk with one blanket neatly folded across it. "You go ahead and sit down there," he says, pointing to the folding chair, the only seat there is. Chuck finds a spot on the ground, crossing his legs.

Ada stares at the chair.

"Don't be such a Yankee."

She takes a seat.

If Ada met Chuck up north she would have mistaken him for someone whose favorite book is *Helter Skelter*, someone who listens to hair metal bands. She would have thought he was someone who wouldn't care if a bit of scrambled egg fell between the stove and the cabinet. He'd leave it there for years. But here, she likes him. "How come people aren't catatonic with wonder?" he asked her once when a scarlet ibis walked through the yard on long yellow backward-bent legs.

Anyway, Chuck would never eat scrambled eggs.

He explained his theory to her when they first met. "Food is fifteen percent nutrients, eighty-five percent poison. Everyone knows it's true but most people just keep on eating. I can't do it. It fogs up my brain when I have a sandwich."

"Really?"

"Yup. People in government keep a different food source. They give us this stuff to make us slow in the body, slow in the head. I won't eat it. You shouldn't either."

"Don't you get hungry?"

Chuck set his mouth in a way that let her know her question was the stupidest question he'd ever heard. Ada stopped poking his precarious foundation.

Ada and Chuck are the same height and the same age, closing in on forty-five. Both are skinny with crab-long limbs and slightly stooped shoulders. Chuck's hair is shoulder-length and thin, hanging feathered from his face like a beach bum's. His head is tanned, skin coarse. Every day he wears Bermuda shorts, bright tube socks, and basketball sneakers. The sneakers remind Ada of things boys said in high school: sweater puppies, butterface, pearl necklace. The sneakers are creepy on a grown man, but Chuck gets his wardrobe from a Catholic Worker center where they hand out food and clothes to unfortunates on Saturdays.

Chuck is not technically unfortunate. He could live with Patricia if he wanted to. Instead he lives in his shed, seeing his sister only on Sundays when they sit together in her air-conditioning to watch reality TV, the green anarchist and the real estate lawyer. He probably does his laundry at her house, using one of her scented dryer sheets. He probably has a snack, something really poisonous like a Pop-Tart or a Slim Jim or an Oreo cookie dipped in Fluff, Jif, Reddi-wip.

"Does Patricia have a boyfriend?" Ada jerks her chin toward the main house, a dark thing with a large wrap-around porch. Ada has only met Patricia once, though she'd spied her before, having a drink alone underneath yellow bug lights on the porch.

"I don't think so. I don't think she likes men. If you know what I mean."

Ada says nothing.

"I don't think she likes women either. She likes her job. And God." He finishes his beer. "You want another?"

For the first time that day the sky suggests the trouble coming from out at sea. The wind begins to pick up, blowing a bit of sand and dirt around. The world gets darker. "Sure."

In between songs, the radio is relating a top-forty list of the world's most destructive natural disasters. Andrew.

Pompeii. Galveston. Katrina. Then, "I Just Called to Say I Love You." There's no rain yet. They sip their beers.

"I heard that maybe one of the reasons we're having so many storms now is because we cleaned up the environment too much. Pollution used to keep the bigger storms in check."

"Well, you heard bullshit." End of that conversation. "Any luck on the job hunt?" he asks.

"Nope." Ada hasn't done much since moving south. Each morning she wakes and has a cup of coffee in her living room. The cup empties and Ada moves out to the lanai to watch the ibises and the lizards. She'll apply a self-tanner to her legs or follow a square of sunlight as it travels across the wall.

"Most people move because of a job," he says, as if Ada were from outer space instead of Rhode Island and he's charged with explaining how humans live, what their customs are.

"Not me."

"No." Chuck lifts his eyes, revealing a field of white below his pupils. He draws his knees into his chest and looks around himself slowly, to the left and right. "So why'd you come here?"

A body trapped in a burlap sack, the answer squirms. "I already told you."

One night they sat together drinking until it was dark and Ada told him her reasons for moving. "I had a fiancé who died," she said.

"I know. Your fiancé. But didn't that happen years ago?" Ada has only been in Florida for a few months.

She hesitates. "It took me a while to get packed."

"All right." Chuck picks at the vegetation underneath his legs. "Shoot," he says, and then, "All right."

"Thanks for the beers." Ada stands. "I'll see you after the storm?"

"You know they've called a county-wide evacuation?"

Ada nods.

"You can just follow the blue signs out on the highway. Head west."

"You're not going to evacuate?"

Chuck looks over at Patricia's house. It's built like an Austrian chalet, a fortress.

"I'll think about it." Ada waves, passing back through the palm trees to her own house, the one with all those windows and nothing but a crawl space for a lost python underneath it.

The red light on Ada's answering machine is blinking. Rhode Island. Foreign grunts from a lost civilization. No one in Florida even knows the number yet. She ignores the message. She has a seat on her new couch, watching the wall of windows as if the feature presentation is about to start there. She eats crackers and peanut butter while she waits. The room darkens some and time passes. The answering machine continues to blink. Outside, branches move in two directions at once, then three directions, shuddering. More time passes. Ada smooths the fabric of the upholstery and the hurricane beats the ocean with 120 mph winds. The lights flicker and brown for a moment, holding the world in pause until the full force of the storm and the sea arrives on cue.

Rain pours down the glass onto the lanai. More time passes. More rain falls. The wind across the roof and gutters snarls while any light left in the sky drains away. Some of the first debris to come flying by the windows is the gray, lower branches of ungroomed palm trees. They are brittle and snap off easily. Their palms act as sails. It's *The Wizard of Oz* out there. A number of store circulars and plastic shopping bags fly past. Ada watches for something heavy and terrible, the neighbors' aboveground pool, a backyard grill, one of the ATVs. She waits for an eighteen-wheeler to drop into her front yard, but the wind is not quite strong enough yet to lift anything heavier than paper, plastic, and dead foliage.

She presses the flashing red button of her answering machine.

"Hi, A. It's me." A friend from Rhode Island. "I didn't want you to hear it from anyone else, but Henry's wife is pregnant. About seven months now. Give me a call." Then a dial tone. In the dark, she smells the rot of those words. Henry's wife is pregnant. The storm grows. Ada shuts her eyes.

"Hello, sweetheart." Flashes of black-and-white light behind her closed lids. A squiggle on a static-filled monitor. "Hello, sweetheart."

And when she opens her eyes the power is gone. The clock on the stove is dark and the lamp switch spins around with no results. When she stands, she sees a small stream now running through her backyard, cutting veins in the sandy soil. It flows directly underneath Ada's house, in one side and out the other. How did that much water get there so quickly? She's never seen rain like this before. Ada bends her ear to the floorboards, listening for the rush of water below, but instead she hears a knock. "Come in," she tells the flood.

"Are you all right over here?"

"Chuck?" It's only been two hours, maybe three, since she last saw him, but the world's changed.

"Yeah."

He's soaked through. He removes his sneakers and socks in the front hall. "Why don't you get your things together and come over to Pat's? You're about to get washed out to sea."

"Man," Ada says. "Look at you. You want a towel?" She passes through her bedroom and into the master bath with Chuck following, dripping throughout the house, accustomed to living where the floors are made of sand.

In the bathroom he twists the fabric of his shorts, wringing dampness out onto the tiles. There are two facing mirrors. Chuck moves his arm and a million arms move with him, replicated into infinity. His tanned skin, his surfer hair, his kooky conspiracies that at first don't make any sense, until quite suddenly they do.

There are four or five drops of water making their way down Chuck's face, beading up into larger drops, waiting to fall but then not falling. "This is some storm," he says, twisting his shorts again. "We never had this many big storms in one season when I was a kid."

She passes him a towel. Chuck holds it but doesn't use it. "That's what they say."

"And Patricia doesn't even believe in global warming."

One drop swings like a charm from the end of his nose. Still he doesn't use the towel.

Chuck raises the timbre of his voice to imitate his sister. "'God won't let us die.' That's what she says."

It's impossible. The drop can't continue to hold on.

"I tell her that God lets us die every day. I don't even know what she's talking about."

It's unbearable, hanging off the very tip. Ada takes the towel and presses it up against him, both her hands open on his face. She holds it there, blotting him out. Ada can feel the cartilage of his nose through the towel, the warmth of his exhalation. She feels his cheekbones and the moisture off his skin. She removes the towel and there, he is dried.

He smiles, stops. "Why'd your fiancé die so young?"

She drops the towel. As with a lie told in childhood, even Ada has forgotten it's a lie. "Terrorists," she says, and begins to smile until she sees how that word tears through Chuck's face, corroded blood or black ink.

"Are you fucking kidding me?" he asks.

But Ada does not have a good answer. So she pulls him to her. She tilts her neck, smelling Chuck's metallic breath. She lifts her chin and Chuck follows, bending to the opposite side, closing in on her. When they'd been together before, it was a mistake, malt liquor, and she had told Chuck the following day, "Not with the neighbors." But here in the hurricane Ada opens her mouth. She silences him. He grabs her quickly with plodding hands, baseball mitts moving across her back.

She's glad the sneakers are already removed when they make their way through the near-dark room and onto her bed.

Her nose presses against his skin. Yeast and old newspapers. A wrong smell. Chuck is a wrong shape also, like a tall, thin chest of drawers. Their bodies do not fit together. Still, she tries. She wraps her arms around him. She moves more out of memory than tenderness. She hitches her leg across him, tearing into him. "Shh. Shh. Shh."

Chuck is clean shaven, which means a bowl of cold water and a razor, grooming himself in a shed without proper plumbing. A gentle action. Two people who live their lives alone in rooms doing strange, gentle things can sometimes be together in the middle of a dangerous storm in a house made of glass. "Shh. Shh. Shh."

"Mercy," he says, arcing his thinness above her. "Mercy."

Ada hasn't any idea why he should ask for mercy.

When it's over they lie on their backs breathing, staring up into the storm though they can't see it. Just a white ceiling with one small crack in the left corner by the doorjamb. She brushes Chuck with her thigh. Maybe the wind will rip the roof from its joists. Or she could just destroy the order of the world. She does it all the time.

Chuck stands and two perfume bottles on her bureau click together. He's naked in front of her. "I'd be curious to hear what you think about it."

By "it" she really hopes he doesn't mean his lovemaking prowess. There are mysterious splotches on his torso like some rare infectious disease.

"I mean when it first happened, were you surprised? I wasn't. We've been asking for it for years."

He's talking about the planes, the buildings. "Oh." Ada pulls the sheet over her head.

"It's a war," Chuck says. "But I don't mean terrorism. I mean capitalism. If you're going to set up hierarchies where one person has very little and another person has a lot more, that's war. Then you're asking for it."

Ada is perfectly flat under her sheet in the gray light. Her eyes dart back and forth, as if some way out, a secret tunnel, might appear beneath the covers. The wind is so loud she can pretend she doesn't hear Chuck.

"Of course nature and the environment are always the lowest man on the totem pole. No one looks out for nature under capitalism because trying to persuade an American to not want more, to stop buying things when they feel badly, is like trying to persuade a person to stop breathing."

She sees her chest rise and fall below the sheet. She hears Chuck pacing at the end of the bed, delivering his fiery sermon.

"When it happened I thought now America will wonder why we'd been attacked and then we'd see how capitalism failed us, how it kills people every day. Cancer, hunger, obesity, heart disease, alcoholism, car crashes." Chuck drives a fist into his other palm. He tallies more casualties. "Genetically fucked-up corn, tobacco, kids on antidepressants, diabetes, asthma, drugs, pollution. This is what American capitalism manufactures. This is our GNP."

The window screen in the bedroom sucks in and out as if it will tear. Something heavy strikes the bathroom skylight. Chuck stops. Ada sits up at the noise. She lets the sheet fall. Her spine curls to a curve. Her boobs touch her stomach. Chuck's nude body makes the trace of a ghost in the room. Here in the storm it's easy for her to see how rigid his spine is. Ada slouches even farther.

"Why was he there?" Chuck asks. "I thought you said you guys lived outside Providence."

Ada focuses on the individual fibers of tan carpeting. And just then, thoughts she'd left back in Rhode Island arrive as if they'd been delayed by careless movers who came south via Alaska. "We're here. Sorry we're late." Ada's lungs slam shut. She sees Chuck's splotchy skin and imagines she's burning those red spots into his flesh with just her eyes, as if the power of her thoughts could hurt someone.

"Hello, sweetheart," she'd said to the ultrasound machine. The Rhode Island obstetrician rubbed jelly across Ada's belly, then turned on the device so that an image appeared on the monitor. A tiny creature swimming inside Ada, its heart beating as fast as a hummingbird. The baby swam. Ada reached her hand out to touch the screen, stroking the black-and-white image there, petting it. A tiny spine, a tiny stomach, the bones of the baby's small feet. Ada could feel the warmth of the monitor underneath her hand as if it were her baby's blood. "Hello, sweetheart. Hello."

She moves quickly, finding her clothes at the base of the bed. A long-sleeved T-shirt, a jean skirt, slip-on leather sandals. She dresses. "Excuse me," she says without waiting for Chuck's answer. Ada closes the door behind her and, using a chair from her dining set, catches the bedroom door handle underneath it, wedging the chair, locking the door shut, just like they do in the movies.

"Chuck?" She speaks to him through the door, fingering the wood of it. "Try the door."

"Huh?"

"I locked you in there."

He tries the door handle and the chair holds. "Why?"

She listens.

He's quiet for a long time except for his breathing. "Oh," he says. "I shouldn't have said that about capitalism killing more people than terrorism. To you. I'm sorry."

"Chuck. You don't know anything," she whispers.

"I know there's no such thing as Us versus Them. I know we want to blame someone so we look around, find a person who is not Us and point the finger. We ask, where'd all that violence come from? Not us, we say. It was them. But they are us, Ada. A better question is where does violence really come from? Don't tell me Cain and Abel. Don't tell me evil, Ada. That's bullshit. There's no such thing as evil." He pauses a moment. "I'd like to ask you, what's the difference between a hurricane and a terrorist attack?"

She leans up against the door. "Is this a joke?"

"No joke. What's the difference?"

Ada doesn't say anything so Chuck answers for her. "Not much for the people who don't survive."

Her head is pressed on the jamb. "Can you try the door once more? Really try it."

"What in the shit are you doing?"

"Just try. Please."

He shoves, backs up and shoves again, like he's getting mad, ramming his shoulder against the wood. The door holds. The chair legs are caught solidly in a crevice between tiles. "I've never done that before."

"Trapped a man in your damn bedroom?"

"Used a chair to lock a door."

"Well, fuck. Congratulations," he says. "I'm not sure what to tell you. Okay," he says. "Okay."

"Chuck." She whispers it, leaning into the door. "Can you hear me?"

He waits a moment. "Yeah."

She bites into her lip without cutting it, just enough to make the pain shoot down her legs and into her toes. She lowers her voice even further. "I want to tell you something."

"All right. Yeah. Tell me." He lets out his breath.

"Terrorists didn't kill Henry. He was nowhere near 9/11. That's just what I tell people."

Chuck is quiet. Ada pictures him still naked on the other side of the door.

"They didn't?"

"No."

"Then who did?"

Chuck could always just climb out the window. He's not really locked in. He just doesn't know he's free. "I did," she tells him and backs away from the door, noticing how, after that, Chuck has very little to say.

The new stream has swollen. It's crested above the lanai. Muddy, debris-filled water is rushing up against the windows. Bending low, Ada looks through the glass. Minuscule grains of sand and dirt glisten. The whole storm in miniature swirls there, tiny golden grains floating in the brown water. The world moves forward in small sudden moments: a phone call from the human resources department, an icy road in winter, a shotgun, a diagnosis. Our existence in the miniature. Each bite of food. Each teenage heartache. The brown flecks in the water. The little baby who never even had a name. Lizards, kingbirds, bugs. But mostly the little baby whose death didn't mean anything to anyone because it happened on such a large and horrible day.

Ada hadn't killed anybody, not even Henry. She'd only wanted to, longing for a bit of violence that would set the world right. Henry's alive and well back in Rhode Island. Still married to his wife, about to become a father.

"Pregnant?" Henry'd said to Ada. "That was not part of the deal."

But Ada never realized there was a deal.

"Pregnant?" he'd said. "That's just about the stupidest thing you've ever done," as if it had occurred immaculately. Henry left and didn't come back and didn't call or even seem to wonder what happened to the baby she was growing inside her. It wasn't immediate, but soon Ada started having evil thoughts about Henry. Hunting accidents, car wrecks, and, though he was too young for a heart attack, Ada wished he wasn't. Garden shears through the lungs, tractor mishaps, poison, each imagined death torturous and deserved.

She hadn't meant to fall in love with a married man. Ada hadn't even known Henry was married until they'd been together for months, and then it was too late because up north falling in love is like animal husbandry. It's necessary. It's so cold in the winter.

She's going to explain this all to Chuck later. She'll tell him about Henry, who was never her fiancé. She'll tell Chuck that she had a miscarriage on 9/11 and it meant nothing to anyone but her. She'll tell Chuck how small each life is when she's ready to tell the truth. Soon she'll let Chuck out of the bedroom and tell him how once it snowed for eight days straight in Rhode Island. She'll tell him how she and Henry would go grocery shopping together and if Henry ran into someone who knew his wife, he'd always pretend that he was just helping Ada out, as if there were something wrong with her mind, retarded or something, he had to take care of her. The floors of the grocery store would be slick from people tracking slush in on their boots. The cashiers kept their parkas on inside. But Henry'd grip the yellow plastic handle of the cart. His strong hands, his wedding ring, and it seemed he was holding on to the whole world, making things steady and even as breath. Ada would see his hands and consider crying or screaming or throwing canned tomatoes, bricks of coffee at his head. She'd turn toward the shelf. Lightbulbs. She'd read the packages, looking for just the right wattage. She'd look down at the linoleum, swallowing the heat behind her eyes, and all the while Henry would wait patiently, smiling, so full with all he had, a wife *and* a girlfriend. Sometimes she could build up a resolve of hatred for him. *I'll leave*, she'd think, but it would never work. She'd take one look at his camouflage hunting coat and get lost in that familiar pattern and all she'd want to do would be to rent a video, go home with Henry for the rest of her life, and watch dumb movies on TV.

But that didn't happen. Henry didn't want to be a father to her child and he didn't want to get divorced. He left and Ada lost the baby at six and a half months, though two doctors said there was no good reason why she, a healthy woman, should miscarry.

The end table would be just the right weight. She could lift it above her head, let the heft of wood have its way with the glass wall. At first there would be just a small crack, a spiderweb that would creep all the way down to the ground, though soon the force of the flood would break through. The window would crash into her living room, allowing the water to enter. Bits of glass in the brown flood. Water would flow into the house, down the hallways, into the kitchen, a shallow river in her dining room. It would flow up against the new sofa and into the low cupboards that are still mostly empty except for some old cassette tapes that Ada can't even listen to anymore because all she has is a CD player. She'd watch the water make its way through the house and up to the bedroom door. Chuck'll forgive her. He's made for forgiveness.

•

"Sorry," the emergency room doctor in Rhode Island had said.

It was just after nine o'clock in the morning. Ada could hear a number of starlings outside the hospital window, whistling, dive-bombing an old pizza crust.

"Sorry?" Ada asked the doctor. That was what people said when someone was dead, and here was Ada, lying on the gurney, perfectly alive.

Did she want to see the baby's body before the morgue took it away?

Should they call someone, a husband or a boyfriend perhaps?

The doctor rolled his lips, and as he did, a frantic candy striper with perfect timing came running down the hall of the hospital, yelling, "We're under attack! Dear lord!" The voice drew the doctor out of the room.

Ada waited alone. The asbestos ceiling stared back at her.

"Oh my god. Oh my god. Oh my god!" another voice passing by in the hallway said. Ada climbed off the gurney. She held tightly on to her now empty belly and the gauze padding the doctor had put inside her. In the hall people were crying, men and women, cardiologists. People were in pain. She watched them pass. Their breathing was labored, their eyes in shock. It came as a surprise to Ada that all these people should understand how the body of one childless mother is too small a place to hold so much grief. Ada's misery was general and spreading through the hospital, down the corridor, out the emergency doors, and across Rhode Island, across the nation. "My baby," Ada said. Hugs were being offered to techs, patients, administrators on the verge of collapse, everyone weeping for her miscarriage. People huddled around the televisions as if the anchors were going to instruct them in grief management. "Coming up. How to make death stop hurting us. Stay tuned." One nurse held his head in his hands, rocking. Ada walked out into the hall, clasping her gown shut. She stopped to stroke the back of the nurse's head. "I was her mother," she told him, and then repeated her claim on all this grief. "I was her mother."

Ada doesn't lift the end table. She opens the slider onto the lanai and steps outside. In the storm it's hard to look up for long without losing her balance. The rain drenches her clothes, smelling of salt and people. Maybe Chuck's shed will come flying through the sky and land on top of her, leaving just her feet sticking out from under like some crushed witch who won't ever have to tell herself the truth.

The water has dampened Ada's clothes, camouflaging her with the oncoming night, darkening the difference between Ada and every other small thing lost in the hurricane.

The water covers her feet, creeps up her shins. The hurricane above her, big as night. The ground shifting below. Ada stands in the storm. One by one, millions of miniature universes pass her by in the flood, remnants of time and shell and silica. They disappear underneath the house in Florida, no us, no them, but all, each one, going down together.

LOVE MACHINE

Once upon a time two men lived at the bottom of a nuclear missile silo. They were barely men, just out of their teens, yet their job required them to push the button when it came time for nuclear apocalypse. Really there are no buttons. They used the word "button" so civilians, friends, could visualize what they were doing in the missile silo. In actuality, each man would have to insert his own key and turn it. Together they would decide whether or not to destroy the world.

Wayne and Dwight paid attention in alternating shifts, ready to wake the other if the signal to act ever came. They were not allowed to leave the missile silo, and so each night and each day—the sixteen-inch poured-concrete walls made it hard to tell which—they slept locked underground, not too far from the huge hole that cradled a massive warhead loaded and aimed.

When Wayne and Dwight were both awake they either played Nerf basketball on a small court they'd rigged in the control room or shot the bull. They'd discussed the moment they were waiting for. They had decided they would do their duty. They would turn their keys and end the world. But then they would forsake the canned provisions stocked to survive the months after the apocalypse safe in the silo. They thought instead they would turn their keys, open the hatch, climb up to the surface of the earth as she died.

Having settled on that plan allowed Dwight to ask Wayne the big questions, like "Why do you think we're here?" or "Do you believe in God?" or "What are you most afraid of?" Wayne always tried his best to answer Dwight's questions but sometimes he didn't know what to say and the two men would listen to the quiet clicks and whirls that the control console made inside their silo.

The call never came. The keys remained on chains around their necks, never sinking into the dark keyholes that Wayne had spent hours, days, and weeks studying. And then their time in the military was up and then Dwight and Wayne drifted apart as people will. But Wayne remembered.

On their last night in the silo they'd opened up a bottle of sparkling cider to celebrate the end of their orders. Soon they would be seeing the sun again on a regular basis. They would see other people as well, and, while it was a little frightening to leave their secured zone after two years together, they both tried to smile and concentrate on the good that would come from returning to the surface. Dwight and Wayne were close that night in a way Wayne's not been able to recall since, as if there were a small man in Wayne's brain who remembers exactly what happened that last night down in the silo, but whenever Wayne tries to remember for himself the little man says, "Well, I could tell you, but then I'd have to kill you."

What Wayne remembers is that there's no way for two men in America who love each other, but who are not lovers, to touch or even talk about love outside of a gambling win or a sporting event.

This was after ROTC, before the FBI, and now, from time to time, Wayne misses Dwight. He misses having a friend to share the long hours with, to share the waiting. Wayne thinks about Dwight and the Cold War while stuck in a van on an FBI stakeout in the forests of Montana.

He's done all right for himself the past five years at the Bureau, racking up top secret clearances like poker chips. Indeed, Wayne's current assignment, Operation Bombshell, is his own brainchild. Though he'd had help from the Development and Fabrication team who'd built her—even weaving human hair collected from wives and sisters into a wig they'd bleached and, later on, deep-conditioned with a fragrant hot-oil treatment. And there were the guys in Robotics, of course. They'd had a hand in developing her language and mobility functions. And Marc from Explosives. He'd been a big help. Still, everyone at the Bureau generally agrees that she, Operation Bombshell, belongs to Wayne.

And here they are in the Montana woods, she and Wayne, down the road a small stretch from a cabin that belongs to one of the most wanted criminals in all of America. Wayne's been on his trail for so many years now that few at the Bureau believe the guy will ever be caught. That'll be fun when Wayne brings this sucker's charred remains into the lab for dental and DNA analysis. He'll show those hot-dogging agents who joke behind closed doors. He's heard them. He's a surveillance expert, for criminy's sake. "There goes Wayne, down the drain," or "Operation Bumshell," or worst, he's heard his name, "Wayne," followed by an explosion of giggles, his career the punch line.

A branch ticks and scrapes against the roof of the van. Wayne studies the dark speedometer. The van has been made to resemble a pool cleaner's work van, but outside of the surveillance equipment stashed in the back, there is little in the way of high-tech luxury. Wayne rests his feet up on the hard plastic console between the driver's and passenger's sides. He sticks his heel down into the cubbyhole made to hold hot beverages. Leaning back in the van's captain's seat, he rubs at a small swatch that he keeps in his pocket. It is a bit of her skin, a square silicone sample. He raises the skin to his nose, tickling a number of wiry nostril hairs. He inhales her faint plastic scent, recalling moments of bliss, some that transpired mere hours earlier in this van as he smiled and selected an outfit for her to wear, helped her test the charge in her battery pack, stuffed her body cavity full of explosives, and then saluted her as she signed off on her first and last mission with a quick nod and the word "Sir." He'd taught her to be a proper soldier. With remote viewing switched on, he watched her knock on the door of the cabin.

·

"We don't want any!" Ted screams through the bolted door. But Ted isn't a "we." He's just an "I."

In the cabin there's one small window from which he often peers out across the valley, startled by how steadfast the mountains can be. Ted waits for the mountains to move or exhale or erupt. He's got all the time in the world. He could wait all day and nothing would ever happen besides the mountains changing colors with the sun at night. Ted tries to achieve such stillness himself and would be able to if not for an itch he always gets right where his hair parts and the grease of his scalp dredges up a dull ache so that he must scratch the itch or be driven insane.

Ted's been alone for a very long time.

Some nights, as the sky turns pink at sunset, he lies on his back staring out the window. The trees' limbs become a darker shade of black, outlines that resemble huge dendrites of nerve endings against the sky. Some nights he will lie there until there is no light left at all, until one shade of black swallows the subtleties and he is alone lying on his back staring at the square window as though it were a dead TV set.

Other nights he'll spend his time building small bombs, some that are thin enough to slip into the open arms of an envelope.

The knocking hasn't stopped. "We don't want any!" Ted screams again to no effect. He cannot believe someone is knocking on his door. He is a million miles away from any civilization. But there it is, steady and rhythmic; the knocks fall like the footsteps of an approaching giant.

There is a joke in this somewhere, Ted's sure. What dedication. The knocking continues at a regular pace for thirty, thirty-five minutes. No kidding. He almost can't believe a passion so unparalleled. This knocker is no quitter, or else, he thinks, this knocker is a robot. Ha! He laughs, finding the joke. A robot in the wilderness of Montana. It's not a very funny joke, not really a joke at all, but he laughs anyway.

"Go away!"

The knocking continues. Ted lies on his back smelling the pine from the floorboards. It is a plague of knocks, a Chinese water torture of knocks. He turns his cheek down to the rough boards. The corner of his lip touches the wood. He curls his body and counts the seconds between each pounding, waiting for the following thud to arrive so that the sliver of silence, the moments between each knock, swells into a room where long, long years of thought are stored, warehouses filled with stalled breaths.

He tries to remember the last time he encountered a human being. *Late last month? I believe so. I went to town for batteries and Fruit Roll-Ups and the woman behind the cash register said, "Will that be all?" and I nodded my head, meaning yes.*

Knock.

Ted doesn't really like people. He prefers the woods, the cabin, and the long dirt road one has to take to get here. The road is overgrown in part with berry bramble that scratches at any vehicle. In some places dead branches fall across the road and he just leaves them there rotting, blocking passage. Such a road is necessary to feel the way he does—that society, if it has to exist, is best kept far, far away, some sort of rare outcropping or singular species of palm tree or hermit crab or saltwater estuary—something that is, but just isn't here, not in the Montana woods.

Ted opens his eyes. The last rays of the sun shine in through the window. The knock comes again. Who is it? He can't imagine. It isn't a postman because he doesn't receive any mail. He makes sure of that by not having a mailbox. Why should the United States government be allowed to come to his house every day except Sunday, to deliver strychnine printed in four-color?

Knock.

No one even knows he is here except for his brother and his brother would not knock.

America moves so quickly it blurs itself into a coma. Ted moves slowly and nothing gets past him. He lifts his spine from the wooden floor like a cobra lifting its head, one vertebra at a time, alert.

Knock. The curiosity's the killing part. He hoists himself up off the floor. He does a quick duck and roll over to the door and, peering through a crack, he sees something that surprises him. He slides back the bolt. He answers his door, something he's never done before.

"Finally," she says, and grabs at her chest as though they are pillows she is trying to fluff. "I thought you had died."

"What?" he asks, and nothing else.

"Well," she says, beginning to explain. "You're not going to believe this," she says as he starts to close the door on her, regretting having opened it. "Wait, please." The door continues to close. "WAIT!" The door stops.

"What?" he asks again.

"They're chasing me. Please."

"Who?"

She looks over her shoulder. "The bad guys."

"Why?" he asks.

"Because I've been a very naughty girl," she says flatly, sincerely, no innuendo.

Ted is puzzled. He is curious. "What'd you do?"

"I shot a man in Reno just to watch him die."

"Huh?"

"He was a U.S. marshal," she says, and her words work. Something turns in Ted. He doesn't care for U.S. marshals either. He doesn't care for the entire U.S. government.

"Do I know you?" he asks her with his arm across the doorjamb, blocking her entrance.

"Don't you want to know me?" She cocks her elbow out to the side and places her hand on her hip, accentuating its curve. She winks and then stomps, a racehorse waiting to run from the starting gate. Her feet are shod in a small pair of steel-toed work boots. The boots look bulky and cut a strange angle to her skin-tight jeans. The boots are a klutzy, confused cousin to her gorgeous hips. He stares. He's never seen a woman like this. Her message becomes vibrantly clear. Everybody needs somebody.

"So can I come in?" she asks.

He steps back. He lets her inside.

"Well." She dusts her hands off on her thighs, stepping through the door and taking a look around the small room. "That's much better."

There's something strange about the way she speaks.

It's both startling and attractive. "Are you from Florida?"
Ted asks. Something about her seems brand-new.

"Florida?" she asks. "Nope!" The tips of her lips curve
into a smile.

Her lips are perfect. Her skin is perfect. Or at least the
skin Ted can see underneath her flannel top and jeans. The
skin glows, like a waxworks he once saw of Brigham Young
and the early pioneers in a Utah rest area. Her skin is so
smooth it looks as though it had once been liquid and then,
when it found the place that was just right, it hardened
up into skin, a pond in winter that freezes before the first
snow. Or maybe it's just been a while since Ted has seen a
beautiful woman.

"Listen, I don't need any trouble. I've got enough,"
he says.

"I won't give you any. I just need a place to hide out for
a few days."

Ted considers his cabin. No one would find her here
and he does like the way she speaks plainly. He trusts her.

"And in the meantime," she says. "Vroom. Vrooom.
Maybe I can get your engine started."

This comment makes Ted blush until, in a moment
of confusion, he starts to wonder whether she means the
broken-down generator he keeps outside the door.

She makes herself comfortable, puts some water on the
cookstove for coffee. She knows how to use a cookstove and
he likes that about her. He likes the way she sets right to
work, fussing in the kitchen. Once she's got the kettle on,
she looks at him again. "Vroom. Vrooom," she repeats, and

walks toward him, slowly twisting each hip. She wraps her finger around his forearm.

"Oh. Oh," he says. "My." Ted is surprised at being touched. Normally the most suspicious man in Montana, he thinks that she is cute with her steel-toed boots. Still, he ducks away from her, because just at that moment he notices his box of fuses and wires plus an empty container of ammonium nitrate have been left out in the open on his worktable. The kettle whistle blows. She turns her back for a moment to brew the coffee, and Ted takes that brief window of opportunity to lift a grungy serape that had been draped across the back of an old bench. He throws the serape over the table where he often sits to think and sometimes sits to build mail bombs he addresses to poisonous technologists.

"Coffee?" she asks. She didn't notice a thing.

"I'd love a cup. Thank you." Ted hardly knows the words to say, it has been so long since he has had a conversation.

She winks at him again. "Why don't you and I get to know one another in the old-fashioned way," she proposes. "Over a cup of coffee."

"Good idea."

"Let's talk. You first." She sits down on the old bench and pats the spot beside her.

"Me?" He takes the cup of coffee from her outstretched hand. She nods. "Okay. Me." He has to think before he starts. "There's not much to tell. I grew up in a house that wasn't too big or too small. It was just right. Son of a sausage maker. Perfectly plain."

"Go on," she says, and bats her eyes, which he notes have lashes nearly as long as the kicker on a stick of dynamite. "I'm enchanted," she says. "Enthralled."

"In junior high I nearly won a Scrabble tournament."

"Fascinating." She leans back, stretching her arm out along the top of the bench, creeping a hair closer to him.

"It's hard to remember much else," he says and looks up to the window, surprised and a bit winded by really how few details it can take to make a life and how difficult it is for him, at this minute, to recall how he's spent his years so far.

"I do remember one thing that was special. I was a kid. I was sitting on the curb outside our house and the macadam road was hot. I remember the heat rising off that blacktop felt like . . ." Ted stops and smiles at her, doing his best Kris Kristofferson. "Felt like a religious experience. I sat there staring straight ahead, perfectly pleased with life on earth, wanting and needing nothing. I lay back." Ted sips his coffee and continues.

"Then two kids from across the street came out and started to lob tiny stones, tiny kernels of asphalt at my stomach. I didn't move a muscle. They laughed. I think they called me names, but after a few minutes they walked on. I still didn't move. I stared straight up at the sun and I felt like if I concentrated hard enough I could sink down into the street, become something solid and hard, like the blacktop road. I lay there all day and when I finally sat up, I saw how I'd gotten burned, a sunburn that left a perfect white silhouette of my hand and fingers on the skin of my thigh just below the fringe of my cutoff shorts. Burned by the sun."

"You're a wonderful storyteller," she says, and blinks her eyes languidly like an engine slowing down.

Ted considers her comment. He's never seen it that way because he's never really had someone to tell stories to, but now that she mentioned it he thinks that his work building bombs, rigging wires in a pattern, constructing paths as tangled and perfect as the trail left by a worm in wood—it all makes a narrative. The red wires lead to the blue wires lead to the trigger, which leads to the black powder. His bombs are masterpieces of storytelling. Sadly, no one ever gets to actually read these stories—that is, except, perhaps, for the scientist who might catch one glimpse before the story blows a hole right through his brain. Worm-eaten.

In the van Wayne taps his fingernail against the plastic casing of his surveillance headphones. He could listen to her talk all day. Her awkward, unknowing way with language. How she accents the wrong syllable. It's adorable.

The Bureau thought of everything. She has a nearly complete digestive and excretory system. She has beautiful baked white enamel teeth that can bite and chew. She even has a saliva simulator. Her anatomy is complete and flawless. Her ears curl like a baby's. She's beyond perfection; she's more than a woman. She's ageless. Her thighs will always be tight, her cheeks will stay soft and moderately blushed even if her batteries still sometimes require quick catnaps to recharge.

Through the headphones Wayne listens to her speak

with Ted. He listens to her charm that scumbag. He looks through the camera that is in her eyes as he remotely commands her to romance this criminal, to demurely cast her gaze down. Wayne looks through her eyes and there, beyond her bosom, he sees her fingers laced within this public menace's thick, dark digits.

Once, down in the silo, Wayne and Dwight had been discussing their onerous nerdy names. Dwight was in honor of Eisenhower and Wayne, Wayne Newton. They laughed at how together, they made Dwayne, but as their laughter died, Dwight asked, "Wayne, have you ever been in love?" It was the sort of question they liked to lob at each other down in the hole.

"Not yet," Wayne answered. "How about you?"

Dwight had his boots up on the console. "Yes. Yes, I have," he replied.

"What does it feel like?" Wayne asked him, and for once Dwight had no answer. Instead his gaze dashed around the silo. His eyes rested on the steel-reinforced concrete wall poured sixteen inches thick, then the bank of walkie-talkies, the hazmat suits hanging empty, the cache of survival rations stacked neatly on an aluminum shelf and arranged by ingredient. Chicken à la King, Dried Tuna Noodle, Chipped Beef. Safety. Wayne waited for Dwight to answer. Dwight stared at the console and its blinking lights, its potential to start a nuclear war. Danger. Finally Dwight answered. "It feels a lot like this, Wayne."

In the cabin Ted tells her, "When I close my eyes I see a revolution as mesmerizing as any rainbow. People will stop and stare as factories, research universities, come tumbling down. People will die, that is for certain." He turns to her and blushes. He doesn't usually speak in metaphors and wonders what sunshine has come over him. "There is a poison in the blood and leeches aren't going to do the trick."

"Hey, what are you so angry about, big boy?"

"You could say I don't like technology."

"What, not even video games, TV?"

He doesn't answer her question. "Imagine that I am a machine."

There's silence in the cabin while she tries to obey his command. She blinks twice.

"Machines," he continues, "have one of only two choices. Either they are run by humans or else they run themselves. And the way I see it, either choice is no good for me. If machines are run by humans, the government and the elite class take over and kill the rest of us off because they don't need worker bees anymore—they have the machines. And if the machines run themselves, they take over and kill all of us. I mean, of course they do. Who doesn't know that? Machines always beat the people who resist them. Take cars as your example. Say you resist the automobile. Say you walk everywhere. You still have to obey traffic signals. You can't cross the road wherever you'd like to, because the machines have won. Try to walk into New York City. Try crossing Route 80. You can't. Machines become responsible for doing every job we humans were put on earth here to do, and what does that leave me?"

"I don't know, sailor boy, what?"

"Not much. A handful of antidepressant pills to pop, pills that were made by the machines in the first place to keep us from revolting."

"I don't know, sailor boy, what?"

"Huh?"

"I don't know, sailor boy, what?"

"What the heck are you talking about?" Ted asks and grabs her shoulder. They'd been getting along so well.

"Fascinating," she says, and then rather suddenly, rather robotically, "I've become extremely tired. I must take a nap." With that she closes her eyes, brings her chin to her chest, and begins to snore. Powerful exhales stir the fringe of the serape that's covering Ted's bomb-building materials.

Poor thing, Ted thinks. *She's been on the run. She's exhausted. I'm tired too*, he thinks. He has also killed people and injured many more. He tries not to think about it too much, but a person has urges. He'll tell her this when she wakes, natural urges to defend ourselves when under attack. He's being attacked by machines. He's being attacked by the government. And who is he to go against nature? Who is she? A person has urges. Yes, a person does, and as if to demonstrate this Ted cups her breast in the palm of his hand and squeezes once while she sleeps. He removes his hand. But there is no tenderness left in him and the experience is not as soft as Ted remembered it once was when he was young. He lets her be. He stares out the window for a while until quite suddenly, after five minutes or so, she flinches before sitting up quickly, stiffly.

"I've been thinking about what you said." She cocks

her head toward him, fully awake. "And I have a question for you."

"What is it?" Ted asks.

"Where do you put beauty?"

"Beauty?"

"Yes," she says. "Beauty. Imagine a small green pond somewhere in the mountains of Montana. There, in the middle of this cool, clear water floats a man, legs together, arms stretched out to the sides like a bird lit from within. The man glows from the green of the water."

Ted pinches his lips in consideration.

She continues. "Machines have made it possible for humans to concentrate on beauty."

"The man glows?" Ted asks.

"Yes, metaphorically."

"Is that man supposed to be me?" he asks.

She shrugs. "Well, I don't see how it could be if you're going to be so busy tending your crops or tilling your fields or walking for three days into Missoula."

Ted sinks his head below the plane of his shoulders. He tucks his chin. He feels like a simpleton for forgetting beauty. "But there's no beauty in machines, and anyway, all those people whose lives have been *simplified* by machines, they don't spend their days concentrating on beauty. They watch TV. Right? What do you think?"

She shrugs again, because in truth she doesn't think. She can't think. She's not built to think. She's just a highly evolved robot, packed with explosives, ready to serve the USA on her only mission.

•

Wayne is listening in the van. He has a timetable, a plan for this criminal scumbag. He'll let Ted go all the way. Wayne wants Ted to know just how good a machine can feel inside. She feels good. Wayne can attest to just how good she feels. He'd volunteered to run Authenticity and Quality Control on her. R&D. Plus there'd been other times, special moments indeed. Yes, she feels good.

The sun has set, and under the darkening sky Wayne dares to pull the van up closer to the cabin to get a better look. He watches through the windshield. Inside they turn on a light. A golden glow creeps out through the one high window. Yellow light makes a cold home into a palace, especially to someone waiting outside alone in a van, his thermos of coffee having long ago cooled. The sky slips from royal to navy blue. The black branches look like a secret army lying in wait, bayonets raised to the sky. Wayne opens the van door and steps out into the dark.

He remembers the Robert Frost he'd been made to memorize in grade school, two roads diverge in a yellow wood. Yellow wood? Maybe yellow's not the right word. Yellow seems odd for a wood. He can't be sure now, but he liked the poem so much he selected it as his high school senior quote in the yearbook. And so he is surprised to find that, here in Montana, years and years later, two roads are diverging. "Turn the key, Wayne," and the other that asks, "Have you ever been in love?" He squeezes the swatch of skin he keeps in his pocket. *Yes.*

Wayne creeps up to the cabin. He hears movement inside and voices, friendly voices, spots of laughter. He presses his ear directly up to the rough siding, a doctor listening through a stethoscope for traces of lung disease or heart irregularities. She's enabled her debating software. Jealousy wells up in him. He holds his breath.

Ted looks up from his teepeed fingers while she speaks.

"So you want me to plant a vegetable garden instead of just going down to the grocery store? Or do you want me to live off other people's trash? Dig through the garbage heap and that will make me happy?" she asks. "I don't think that will make me happy."

"The garden might."

"Yes, it's true. The garden might. Okay. So say we go ahead with your plan, build lots of bombs, kill all the machines. Say we get past the point of revolution, all the cities are gone, the interstates gone, all the strip malls, industrial complexes, and health clubs are gone, and we're all using our bodies to work really hard again, tilling the fields, killing bears with rocks, living off of honeysuckle, building wigwams and igloos, hiding in trees, digging in the dirt for grubs; it still wouldn't matter, because somewhere there'll be a spark in some youngster's brain, someone who thinks, 'Hmm, if I plant an extra row of corn I can sell it to my neighbors. If I build myself a gin I could sure pick a whole lot more cotton.'"

Her perfection is alarming.

"It'll just start all over again," she says.

And, in the cabin, Ted knows she's right. He hangs his head, defeated. He's already thought of that youngster with the big ideas himself. He tried to ignore that youngster. In his head, in his plan, he only saw undulating fields of golden wheat and children playing hide-and-go-seek in the corn. He saw how the woods are the poor man's overcoat with mushrooms, hazelnuts, a soft pine-needle bed, sweet maple sap, and a fire for reducing the sap. So much has already been given to us. He just can't believe people could want more.

"What do you want?" he asks her, and she makes an expression that looks like thinking while her computers search for anything lacking. "Detonation" is all her computers come up with, but that result lies beyond her firewall, along with all the other essential truths about herself that she isn't allowed to reveal, a glitch they'd had to fix after she said too much to that U.S. marshal in Reno. And so her computer instructs her to lie. She answers, "Nothing really. What do you want?"

Ted stops to consider. His mug of coffee has reached the bottom but he doesn't really want a refill. If he has too much caffeine he won't sleep well tonight. He looks around. What does he want?

"Do you want me?" she asks.

But Ted is staring out the window, his theories slipping away from him. He lets her words pile up on his stomach like tiny asphalt pebbles. Beauty, even her beauty, has become something to him like a stone, a solid pit in his chest. His answer would have broken her heart if she'd had one.

"Wayne, you were supposed to detonate me while I was there in his cabin."

"I know."

"You failed in your duty to serve the United States of America, Honor Code section four, paragraph nineteen."

"I know."

"There are consequences," she says.

"I know," Wayne answers, and reaches out to hold her cheek in his hand. She doesn't move away. She is programmed not to resist male advances. He pulls her down onto the floor of the van, beside the pool cleaning apparatus. He nestles his face in her neck. He wraps his hand around her waist underneath her flannel shirt and pulls her closer, feeling the silicone lumps that are her breasts push into him. He smells the chalk of her scent while her arms remain limp by her sides. "Hold me," he commands her, though he feels immediately ashamed, desperate. Still, "Hold me," he repeats. She complies and wraps her mechanical arms around him while he speaks words of loving sweetness into her ear, the ones she's been waiting to hear, hot breath against plastic. Wayne whispers the magic words that send a repressed tremor through the quiet night, an explosion that could only be described as American.

A LOVE STORY

"A coyote ate a three-year-old not far from here."

"Really?"

"Yeah. My uncle told me."

"Huh."

"He said, 'Don't leave those babies outside again,' as if I already had."

"Had you?"

"Come on." An answer less precise than no.

"Why's he monitoring coyote activity up here?"

"Because."

"Because?"

"It's irresistible."

"Really?" Again. A word that means *I doubt your grasp of the truth.*

My uncle's so good at imagining things, like a wild dog with a tender baby in its jaws disappearing into the red-woods forever, he makes the imagined things real. "Yeah."

"Irresistible?"

"It's what he does, a habit." Or compulsion.

"I don't get it," my husband says.

But I do. Every real thing started life as an idea. I've imagined objects and moments into existence. I've made humans. I've made things up. I tip taxi drivers ten, twenty dollars every time they don't rape me.

The last time my husband and I had sex was eight months ago and it doesn't count because at the time my boobs were so huge from nursing that their power over him, over all men really, was supreme. Now, instead of sex with my husband, I spend my nights imagining dangerous scenarios involving our children. It's less fun.

"Watch out," my uncle says. "Watch out," taking his refuge in right-wing notions, living life terrified of differences.

Once, I was a drug dealer, back when pot was still illegal here. I'm a writer now. It's not that different from being a drug dealer. Both have something to do with levels of reality. Both offer flexible hours for mothers. I haven't made any money writing yet; still, that's how I spend my days, putting things down on paper. People continue to come to my house to buy pot and I sell it to them even though I'm no longer a drug dealer and they could get this shit legally and I'm sick of the people who pop their heads in my door, all friendly-like: "Hi. How you doing?"

"Fine," I'll say, but I mean, *Shut up and buy your drugs*

and stop thinking you're better than me. I probably won't have too many customers for much longer. There's got to be a whole lot of people who are better drug dealers than I am.

When I was young I shopped at the Army/Navy with the thought that if I bought these clothes and wore them I would prevent some beautiful young man from being killed in the garments. I'm a romantic. I'm writing about the coyotes, the kids, the taxi drivers, the drugs, and the romantic notions because I want to be as honest as I can. As I said, thoughts become material. I want to make truth. It's too bad I have to say this, but I will: I'm not hysterical or crazy. I'm providing a guided tour to a woman with hormones. Let's talk about differences. Let's lay the groundwork for real honesty, for belief, for biology, for no more *Really?*

I had great hopes the threat of Lyme disease would revitalize our sex life. "Will you check me for ticks?" You know, and things would go from there. Grooming each other as monkeys do. In that way, at least for a while, I got him to touch me again and that felt good, but then Lyme disease never really took off in California like it did on the East Coast.

Most men I know speak about sex as if their needs are more intense or deeper than women's needs. Like their penises are on fire and they will die if they can't extinguish the flames in some damp, tight hole. When I was younger I believed men when they said their desires were more intense than mine because they talked about sex so much through high school and college. I didn't recognize this talk as a prop of false identity. The men developed entire industries devoted to this desire, this identity. The aches! The suffering of the boys! The shame and mutual responsibility for blue balls. The suffering of the boys. *Poor boys*, I thought. *Poor boys*, as if I were being called upon to serve in a war effort, the war against boys not getting any.

Why do people act like boys can't be human? Like they don't control their own bodies? It's not a very nice way to think about boys.

The only desire/constructed identity I have that compares to the way men talk about sex is my devotion to rehashing the past. I relive the exquisite pain of things that no longer exist: my father's jean jacket, my father, Travolta's 1977 dark beauty, how it felt to be alone in the house with my mom after my siblings finally left for school, the rotations of my first record player spinning the Osmonds and Paper Lace, the particular odors of a mildewed tent in summertime. Memory as erogenous zone.

But then I, too, started to burn, and while no one wants to hear about middle-aged female sexual desire, I don't care anymore what no one thinks. There are days I ache so badly, the only remedy beyond a proper plowing, beyond someone using their body to slam all the self out of myself, would be a rusty piece of metal or broken glass to gouge out my hot center from mid-inner thigh all the way up to my larynx. I'd spare my spine, brain, hands, and feet. I'm not irrational.

The list of potential reasons for why my husband and I no longer have sex wakes me up at night. If I'm not already awake thinking about the coyotes. The first reason, the wildest, craziest reason, is that maybe my husband is just gone. Maybe one night a while back I kicked him out after a fight and maybe, even if I didn't mean everything I said, maybe he went away and hasn't come back yet. That would certainly explain why we don't have sex. Maybe I'm just imagining him here still. Thoughts making material, etc., etc. *Really?* etc., etc. It can be hard to tell with men, whether they are actually here or not. Especially a man with a smartphone.

The second reason I develop for why my husband and I no longer have sex is that my husband is, no doubt, gay. A faultless situation, though not without its heartache and deceit.

The third reason I concoct for why my husband and I no longer have sex is that he must be molesting our children when he puts them to bed each night. This reason does a lot of work for me, double duty, cultivating hysterical worry about both my marriage and my kids at the same time. Such efficiency. It is also so insane, so far out to the margin, that some nights it can actually help to reset my brain back to center.

The fourth reason I develop is that now, after pregnancy, I've lost the ability to see myself clearly. My feeling is that I probably look like a chubby Victorian maid: bad teeth, mouth agape, drooling ignorance and breast milk. This reason sends me onto the Internet for hours, researching various exercise regimens and diets hawked by self-tanned women with chemically bruised hair. In the middle of the night it's easy to hate myself as much as the world hates me.

A few years ago my husband bought me a short black wig as part of a sex toy package. His ex-girlfriend has short black hair. I know the chemistry of other people's desire is not my fault, but the wig, so raw, really hurt.

Finally the last reason I imagine for why my husband and I no longer have sex comes almost as a relief because it requires very little imagination or explanation and after I think it, I can usually go back to sleep. My husband must be having an affair.

I have a friend from college, Susan Pembroke. She's a real New England WASP with a fantastic secret. Her family pays for all those Lilly Pulitzers, summers on Nantucket, and boarding schools from a fortune made manufacturing dildos and vibrators. I love that secret. One of their biggest sellers is a set of prosthetic monster tongues, some forked, some spiky, most of them green or blue plastic, all of them scaled for the lady's pleasure, especially ladies with lizard fetishes.

Susan once asked me a greasy question that returns on nights like this one, nights unhinged. "Are you the kind of woman who would want to know if her husband's cheating on her or not?" And she left the question dangling. Her mouth might have even been open slightly. People cheat because we are no longer running away from saber-toothed tigers. I get that. Adrenaline insists on being taken out for a spin. But there was an indictment inherent in either answer I could give Susan, so I stayed silent and wondered, was she asking because she knew something?

•

We moved out of the city because there's no room for non-millionaires there anymore. In the country, life is more spacious. We bought a king-sized bed. Some nights we snuggle like people in an igloo, all five of us. Those nights, our giant bed is the center of the universe, the mother ship of bacterial culture. It is populated with blood, breast milk, baby urine, a petri dish of life forms like some hogan of old. Those nights I know we are safe. But when our children sleep in their own room my husband and I are left alone on the vast plain of this oversized bed feeling separate, feeling like ugly Americans who have eaten too much, again.

When one turns to the Internet for mothering advice, one finds a plague of perfectionism. One could be led to believe that mothering means Alice in Wonderland birthday parties; Spanish-speaking nannies; healthy children harvesting perfect blue chicken eggs from the backyard coop; homeschooled wonders who read by age three; flat, tight bellies; happy husbands; cake pops; craft time; quilting projects; breast pumps in the boardroom; micro vineyards of pinot grapes; ballet tights; cloth diapers; French braids; homemade lip balm; tremendous flat pans of paella prepared over backyard fires. What sort of sadist is running these Internets? And more important, how do these blogs not constitute acts of violence against women?

I glimpsed a huge beyond when I became a mother, the enormity of an abyss or the opposite of an abyss, the idea of complete fullness, the anti-death, tiny gods everywhere. But now all that the world wants to hear from me is how I juggle children and career, how I manage to get the kids to eat their veggies, how I lost the weight.

I will never lose this weight.

When one encounters a mother doing too many things perfectly, smiling as if it is all so easy, so natural, we should feel a civic responsibility to slap her hard across the face, to scream the word "Stop! Stop!" so many times the woman begins to chant or whimper the word along with us. Once she has been broken, take her in your arms until the trembling and self-hatred leave her body. It is our duty.

I used to think it was motherhood that loosens a woman's grasp on sanity. Now I see it is the surplus and affluence of America. Plus something else, something toxic, leaking poison, fear. Something we can't yet see. But not motherhood itself.

I'd like to post some shots from my own childhood, a version of my parents' parenting blog, if such an abomination had existed back then. In every photo through the fog of cigarette smoke filling the living room, across the roar of Georges Moustaki blasting his sorrow from the record player at midnight, it would be difficult for a viewer to even locate the children in rooms so thick with adults acting like adults. Here, I found mystery. There was no fear. Here, I was glad to face the night unprotected.

In my new career as a writer, I've been thinking about drafting a manual for expecting mothers. An honest guide through a complex time no one's ever properly prepared for. After I became a mom I asked an older friend, "How come you never told me I'd lose my identity when I had a kid?"

" 'Cause it's temporary. And I kind of forgot."

"Really?"

"No."

When I sit down to begin my manual I understand how specific my guide is to one demographic. So then, okay, a mothering guide for middle-class, heterosexual women who went to college and are gainfully employed. But once I've arrived there, my pen still lifted at the ready, I realize I actually have very little wisdom. So a brochure. Pen in hand. Until I realize that what I've learned about being a middle-class, hetero mother who went to college could actually be boiled down to one or two fortune cookies. I write, HORMONES MAKE LIFE. HORMONES MAKE MENTAL ILLNESS. I write, EQUALITY BETWEEN THE SEXES DOES NOT EXIST. And then my job is done.

A few days ago I was scrubbing the rim of the upstairs toilet because it smelled like a city alley in August. My phone dinged. I'd received an e-mail. I pulled off my latex gloves to read the message. (Who am I kidding? I wasn't wearing gloves. I was scrubbing the toilet with bare hands. Honesty. I was probably even using the same sponge I use on the sink, for that area right near the toothbrushes.) The e-mail was from my husband. "Thought you might like this," he said. It was a link to a list of something called Life Hacks, simple tricks designed to make one's life easier: use duct tape to open tough lids, keep floppy boots upright with swimming pool noodles, paper clip the end of a tape roll so you can find it easily.

I wrote him back. "Or you could marry a woman and make her your slave."

He never did respond.

I'm not saying men have it better or women have it better. I've never wanted to be a man. I'm just saying there's a big difference.

When I swim at the public pool I wear sunglasses so I can admire the hairless chest of the nineteen-year-old lifeguard. I love it that he, a child, is guarding me, fiercest of warriors, a mother, strong as stinky cheese, with a ripe, moldy, melted rotten center of such intense complexity and flavor it would kill a boy of his tender age.

Once, I woke Sam in the night. That's my husband's name, Sam. "Honey," I said. "Honey, are you awake?"

"Uhh?"

"I think I'm dying."

"Yeah," he said. "Uh-huh," and went back to sleep.

Presumably my husband likes stinky cheese and the challenge of living near my hormones. Presumably that's what love is.

Another night, also in bed, I woke Sam. I do that a lot. "I want you to agree that there is more than one reality."

"Huh?"

"I want you to agree that if I feel it, if I think it, it is real."

"But what if you think I'm an asshole?" he asked.

"Then that's real."

"Really?"

"What's that word even mean, really?" I started to scream a little. "You think we all see things the same way? You think there's one truth and you know it?"

"Sure. Right? Really?" he asked. *Really.*

One huge drawback to my job as a drug dealer is that, while I grow older, passing through my thirties and into my forties, the other drug dealers stay young. They are almost all in their twenties. Normally, I don't socialize with the other drug dealers, but one night a group of the twenty-year-olds asked if I wanted to join them for a drink. I almost said no, but then decided, why not.

All the motions at the bar were familiar. It's not as if I forgot how to go out for a drink. I know how to order a glass of wine. I had no trouble climbing onto a bar stool. After our first drink, some of the young drug dealers disappeared to play pool, some wandered off to greet other friends. Halfway through my second glass, I was holding down the fort alone, watching a couple of purses and cocktails left in my charge. No problem. I didn't mind a moment of silence. Plus, the young drug dealers can sometimes be stupid, boring.

But then a young man, handsome, curly hair, strong hands, joined me at the table. I started to panic.

This, I suddenly thought, is what it means to go out for a drink. This is the entire purpose. Have a drink, meet a stranger, have fantastic sex all night long. But I didn't want to blow up my life. I love Sam. I love our life. Still, there was this young man beside me, interested in me, nervous even.

"Hi," he said. "I'm a friend of Alli's." One of the twenty-year-old drug dealers.

"Hi." I tried not to, but I imagined him naked, me naked. I imagined him accepting the way my body has aged naturally, despite the near certainty that that would never happen. Very few bodies this close to San Francisco are accepted or allowed to age naturally.

"Alli told me you're a mom."

"That's right." It wasn't the sexiest thing he could say, but maybe, I thought, this is how it will work, how he'd come to appreciate the lines and rolls of my abdomen.

"I was thinking, since you're a mom, you might have some snacks? I'm really hungry. Like, is there anything in your purse?"

After a short excavation, the highest humiliation: he was right. I found both a bag of baby carrots and a granola bar in my purse. I passed my offerings across the table to the young man.

"Thanks," he said, disappearing with the food. "Thanks." Some mother's child, some mother who had at least taught her son to always say please, always say thank you.

"Can you check me for ticks?"

Sam switches on a light, picks me over, stopping at

each freckle. How lucky I am to know such love, to momentarily remember what it means to have the body of a child, ignorant of age's humiliation. "Okay," he says. "You're all clear."

"Thanks. Should I check you?"

"Nah. I'm good. There's no Lyme disease in California, hon. Not really."

"Says you."

He switches off the light and now it's night. It is really, really night.

What's the scariest sound a person can hear?

Away from the city, inside a quiet country house where the closest neighbors are pretty far away, the scariest possible sound is a man coughing outside in the dark. Because why is there a man standing in the dark, studying the sleeping house, licking his lips, coughing? Why should someone be so near to my home, to my children, in this place that is not the city?

I know the sounds of this house intimately. The garbage truck, the school bus. I know the difference between the mailman and the UPS man. I know each door. I know the sound of a man outside coughing.

"What was that?" But Sam is already asleep. Or Sam is not here. "Wake up." I whisper so the coughing man won't know we're onto him. "Wake up, hon. Someone's outside."

"What?"

"Shh. I heard something."

"What?"

"There's someone downstairs. Someone's outside."

"Who?"

"A guy. Please."

"Please?"

"Go see."

"See."

"Yeah."

Dead and dark of night, I send away the only man who has sworn an oath to protect me. I must be an idiot. I must be really scared. I send away the man I love. Why am I so scared? It's not like I live in a war zone. It's not like a flesh-eating epidemic has been found in our school district. What makes me so frightened?

Sam disappears in his underwear and bare feet, leaving behind the retired baseball bat he once thought to stow under the bed for just this sort of occasion. The soft pads of his feet pass down the top risers and then there's no more sound. He's so gone I have a sense our entire downstairs is filled with stagnant black pond water through which he's now wading, swimming, drowning, trying to stay quiet so the bad guy, whoever he is, doesn't hear him, find the staircase, and tear our tiny world apart.

The uncertain position we all maintain in life asking when will violence strike, when will devastation occur, leaves us looking like the hapless swimmers at the beginning of each *Jaws* movie. Innocent, tender, and delicious. Our legs tread water, buoyed by all that is right and good and deserved in this world, a house, healthy children, clean food to eat, love. While that animatronic shark, a beast without mercy, catches the scent of blood and locks in on his target.

"Sam?" I call softly so the bad guy won't know we're separated.

There's no answer from downstairs. What is taking him so long to come back?

I hold the night the way I would a child who finally fell asleep. Like I'm frightened it will move. I am frightened it will move. I am always scared my life will suffer some dramatic, sudden change. I try to hear deeper, to not shift at all, to not breathe, but no matter how still I stay there's no report from downstairs. What if Sam is already dead, killed by the intruder? Maybe choked by a small rope around the neck? What if the bad guy, in stocking feet, is creeping upstairs right now, getting closer to my babies, to me?

Part of me knows he is. Part of me knows he always is and always will be.

Where we live there are squirrels, rabbits, all manner of wild birds, foxes, mountain lions. There are rednecks getting drunk at the sports bar three miles away. There are outlaw motorcycle clubs convening. Drunk frat boys.

There are also children dreaming.

Other living things still exist in the night. Sometimes it's hard to remember that.

Sam is probably fine. He's probably downstairs on his computer. Barely Legal, Backstreet Blow Jobs. Looking at some other mother's child perform sex on his monitor.

Night ticks by.

"Sam?" There's no answer and the quiet becomes a dark cape, so heavy I can't move my legs. I can't move my body.

I am only eyes, only ears. The night asks, *Who are you? Who will you become if Sam has been chopped to bits by the guy downstairs?* This is a good question. Who am I? Who will I be without Sam? Without kids? I can hear how well-intentioned people at Sam's funeral will say, "Just be yourself." But there is no self left. Why would there be? From one small body I made three new humans. It took everything I had to make them. Liver? Take it. Self-worth? It's all yours. New people require natural resources and everyone knows the laws of this universe: you don't get something for nothing. Why wouldn't I be hollowed out? I grew three complex beauties. I made their lungs and noses. Who can't understand this basic math?

The strangest part of these calculations is that I don't even mind. Being hollow is the best way to be. Being hollow means I can fill myself with stars or light or rose petals if I want. I'm glad everything I once was is gone and my children are here instead. They've erased the individual and I am grateful. The individual was not special in the first place. And really, these new humans I made are a million times better than I ever was.

The bedcovers look gray in the dim light of modems and laptops and phones scattered around our bedroom. In this ghost light I am alone. The night asks again, *Who are you? Who will you be when everyone who needs you is gone?* My children are growing, and when they are done with that I'll have to become a human again instead of a mother. That is like spirit becoming stone, like a butterfly going to a caterpillar. I'm not looking forward to that.

Who are you?

The answer is easy in daylight. But the night's untethering almost always turns me into someone I'm not. I sift through the different women I become in the dark, my own private Greek chorus whispers, shrieks. Where do I keep all these women when the sun is up? Where do they hide, the women who have breached the sanctity of my home, who know things about me so secret even I don't know these things? Maybe they are in the closet. Maybe they are hiding inside me. Maybe they are me trapped somewhere I can't get to, like in the DNA markers of my hormones, those mysterious proteins that make me a woman instead of something else, those mysterious proteins no one seems to understand.

You may ask, Are these women who bombard me at night real or do I imagine them? You may eventually realize that is a stupid question.

I think about fidelity. To Sam, to myself. The light is still gray. The night is still so quiet. I let the women in, an entire parade of them, the whole catalog, spread out on the bed before me. Sam is gone and these women keep me company. These women are women I need to reckon with, even if some of them terrify me. The light is gray and the night is quiet.

I let the other women in.

CGB5
human chorionic gonadotropin
hormone produced by the embryo after implantation

An author lived for a time in a modern house behind mine, through a eucalyptus grove. She had recently divorced. She is a very good writer, though she has only written one book. The book takes a frank approach to sex and bodies. I try to copy her style in my own writing. I fail. Her book is about prostitutes, so I assume she was once a sex worker. Or maybe she just wants her readers to believe that, street cred at book parties, in university settings, etc.

I could kind of see into the rear windows of her house at night with a pair of binoculars. These voyeur sessions never lasted long because all she ever did was sit there. Maybe once or twice I caught her walking to her kitchen. It was boring. She was alone all the time, and while she was no doubt thinking amazing, fantastic thoughts about the nature of art, my binoculars could not see these thoughts.

The town where we live is small so it was inevitable that we would meet. We did, many times. We once even shared the dance floor at the local bar, a Mexican restaurant, moving together like robots from outer space. But then, each time we met again it was, to her, as fresh as the first time. "Nice to meet you," she'd say. When once I had to deliver a piece of misdirected mail, she invited me in for a glass of wine. In an instant I developed a fantasy of the famous writer and me as best friends. I dropped that fantasy quickly because it was clear that her alien robot routine back in the bar/restaurant had not been an act.

When I mentioned that I had three children, her jaw came unhinged. "Oh my god." Her hand lifted up to her face as if I'd said I have three months to live. Maybe that is what children mean to her. I recalled an interview where she had likened motherhood to a dairy operation, where she said children murder art. She dismissed me after one glass of wine. "I have to eat my sandwich," she said, as if that sandwich was something so solidly constructed it would be impossible to divide, impossible to share. I left.

The next time I saw the famous writer she was in the grocery store. Once again she didn't recognize me or acknowledge the four or five times we'd already met, the wine we had drunk together, so I was able to freely stalk her through the aisles of the store, to spy the items of nourishment a famous writer feeds herself upon: butterfly dust, caviar, evening dew.

I stood behind her in line at the fishmonger's counter, my own cart bulging with Cheerios, two gallons of milk, laundry soap, instant mac and cheese, chicken breasts, cold cuts, bread, mayonnaise, apples, bananas, green beans, all the flabby embarrassments of motherhood that no longer embarrass me. I heard her order a quarter pound of salmon. The loneliest fish order ever. I stepped away, scared her emaciated solitude might be contagious. She kept her chin lifted. Some people enjoy humiliation. Maybe I used to be one of these people, but I don't feel humiliation anymore. The body sloughs off cells every day. So much mortification that, after all that, what is left to feel humiliated? Very little indeed.

THRA1
thyroid hormone receptor
regulation of metabolism and heart rate, development
of organisms

The commuter bus that runs between my town and the city is one small part of America where silence still lives.

It's a cylinder of peace moving through the world swiftly enough to blur it. Some days I ride this bus when I have work to do in the city. Compared with raising children, going to work is extremely easy. I turn off my mind. I eat lunch in silence. I have conversations that follow logical patterns. I stop steering a family as unwieldy as an oil tanker.

Once, on a return bus, there was a woman seated ahead of me. People do not speak on the bus. We understand that this hour of being rocked and shushed is the closest we'll get to being babies again. This woman was not a regular. She'd gone down to the city for the day. She was ten to fifteen years older than me, mid-fifties, though I never saw her face. I could feel her buzzing. She'd taken a risk traveling to the city by herself, such a risk that accomplishing it had emboldened her to try other new things like the voice recognition software on her smartphone, that "newfangled" device purchased for her by an older child who had tired of a mother living like a Luddite.

There was nothing wrong with her hands but she wanted to demonstrate that even though she was middle-aged and less loved now than she'd been in the past, she could be current with the modern world. She could enjoy the toys of the young. On the quiet bus, she began to speak into her phone as if recording books for the blind, loudly and slowly. Everyone could hear. There on the silent bus, the woman shouted multiple drafts of an e-mail to her friend, laying plain her regret, fumes of resignation in the tight, enclosed area.

Hi. Just on my way home. I spent the day with Philip and his glamorous wife. He had a concert at the conservatory. I hadn't been back in years. It was great to see him. His wife is gorgeous. They live in Paris. Ouch. I just

The woman paused and considered. She tried again. Her voice even louder, as if it were another chorus, a building symphony of mortification.

Hi. I'm on the bus back from the city. What a day. I saw Philip. He had a concert at the conservatory. His wife is gorgeous, glamorous, everything I'm not. They live in Paris and their kids

She paused again. Take three. Loud and utterly desperate. Words falling apart.

Saw Philip and his gorgeous wife. Conservatory. Paris. Kids. I just

I turned to the window, which was of course sealed, but at least reminded me what fresh air meant, what it was to breathe without the toilet cabin leaking air freshener, her echoing regret.

ESR1
estrogen receptor
sexual development and reproductive function

People should be more careful with their language. People shouldn't infect innocent bystanders with their drama.

There's a man I hardly know, an academic. He began sleeping with a graduate student when his wife was pregnant, but everything was cool because, you know, everyone involved reads criticism and all three of them want to test the bounds of just how much that shit can hurt.

I imagine that shit can hurt a whole lot.

I know a lot of professors who fuck their students, graduate and undergraduate. Every time I hear about another professor with a student I think, *Wow, that professor I know is way more messed up than I ever thought. Stealing confidence from eighteen-, nineteen-, twenty-year-olds.*

Nasty. Vampires.

This professor, he cleared the fucking of the graduate student with his pregnant wife, and for reasons I don't understand yet, the wife allowed him to dabble in younger, unwed women while she gestated their child, while her blood and bones were sucked from her body into their fetus.

Though the wife is an interesting part of this triangle, it's neither she nor the husband I'm thinking of here in bed while Sam bleeds out his last drop of life on our living room floor. I'm thinking of the poor, stupid graduate student.

She and the academic attended a lecture together one night. Though it is a city, almost every person there who identifies as "academic" knows every other person there who identifies as "academic." The city becomes small by types. The academic and the grad student attended a lecture and a party afterward. She was in the insecure position of being a student among people who were done being students. And though everyone was staring at her—they knew the wife—no one wanted to talk to her or welcome the grad student into the land of scholars.

This was not acceptable. She likes attention. She likes performance. She cleared her throat and the noise from the room as if readying for a toast. She stood on the low coffee table. Everyone stopped drinking. Everyone left cigarettes burning. In a loud, clear voice that must still reverberate in her ears, she said, "You're just angry because of what I do with my queer vagina."

On my living room wall I keep a photo of my Victorian great-grandmother engaged in a game of cards with three of her sisters. These women maintained a highly flirtatious relationship with language. "Queer" once meant strange. "Queer" once meant homosexual. "Queer" now means opposition to binary thinking. I experience a melancholy pause when meaning is lost, when words drift like runaways far from home. How did "queer" ever come to mean a philandering penis and vagina in a roomful of bookish, egotistical people? How did common, old, vanilla adultery ever become queer?

I feel the grad student's late-blooming humiliation. How she came to realize, or will one day soon, that her words were foolish, creating an unwanted idea of an organ, her organ, that, like all our organs, is both extraordinary and totally plain. Some flaps of loose skin, some hair, some blood, but outside the daily fact of its total magnificence, it is really not queer at all.

CYP17

cytochrome P450 17A1

a key enzyme in the steroidogenic pathway that
produces progestins, mineralocorticoids, glucocorticoids,
androgens, and estrogens

A once-beautiful woman, who married for money, is mean
as a mad dog. She sometimes calls salesgirls cunts. She
has a couple of kids. She might remember a few good years,
but now she hates her husband. She hates her husband's
parents, too. She didn't grow up with money and nannies,
and now that she's wealthy, she can't believe how much the
rich just phone that shit in. She's also mad because, by now,
she's been rich so long that she's completely dumb. She
doesn't know how to do anything anymore. All those years
spent hiring people to do everything for her. She's mad
because her husband, an ugly troll who thinks women make
really good holes for his cash and his dick, uses a high-end
escort to take care of certain desires he's never had the cour-
age to discuss with her, his wife.

Let that mess brew for a few years.

The woman bought a summerhouse by the beach
because it was the most expensive place and she wants her
husband to pay a lot. She takes the kids there from June to
the end of August. That way she's not responsible for any
wife duties: cooking, laundry, pleasantness, napkin folding, buying of gifts, wrapping up gifts, tipping garbage-
men, scrubbing under the rim (not that she would ever
do this), making the bed, dressing the children, doing the
homework, fucking and sucking, making the lunches,

making the coffee. Each summer now she finds herself at the beach, right at the beach, face-to-face with the ocean that, despite having no mercy, is full of judgment. "You married him for shiny things and new cars," it says.

"So."

"At least he was once in love. You're the worst. Shriveled, frigid." The ocean doesn't really speak like an angry Irishman, but she hears it anyway, the way it just keeps rolling and rolling, judging her.

Imagine if even the ocean didn't want you. That would feel very bad. Imagine the ocean refused you entry.

A few hours ago a Volvo or a Land Cruiser driven by a teenager came and stole her children away. "Going out, Mom."

"Where?"

"Out."

She considers the places her children might hide: a drunk house party with no parents, a private dune. She doesn't think ice cream parlor or skinny-dipping. She knows her children are too awful to enjoy something so innocent.

She's alone in the house. The kitchen is in order. To-morrow the Colombian girl will do the laundry. There is no purpose to her life. No one needs her. Nothing to be done. She hears the waves. She hears her son's electronic devices processing distant communications. She drinks more wine, worrying it will make her fat and fatness will cause her entire world to come tumbling down. Then she hears someone laughing.

Next door to her summer home, a civic-minded body of locals, old hippies, collected funds to install four benches looking out to sea. The benches were built by people who live by this beach year-round, an unimaginable position. They got permission in the off-season, as locals will, to place their public benches within clear-sounding distance of her private property.

Alone and empty, she hears voices, drunk, awful locals chatting, laughing, enjoying the benches. She already raised a stink to the town council and had a sign erected that states the benches are only to be used during daylight hours. But the sign is a splendid failure. It is so dark at her end of the street, once the sun sets, no one can read the sign. Nearly nightly now it falls to her to sweep these dregs back to town or whichever lesser view they came from.

Alone in this house, on this far beach with no one to ask, *Do you want to take a walk, do you want to watch a movie, should we head up to bed now,* the laughing continues. Her blood rages. She unseals her window. The night air disturbs her controlled climate. Another trespass these bench sitters claim. She opens her mouth. Violence and pure rage let loose. Fine, thick, rich curse words pour from her mouth, indignities to scratch untouchable itches like Where is her husband? Where are her children? How for fuck's sake did she, a beautiful person, end up in this house, on this beach, with no one?

Her initial tirade is met with silence. "Get out of here!" she screams.

The bench sitters do nothing, they stare openmouthed, a woman with two girls.

"What is your fucking problem? This is my property!" They don't move.

"You stupid shits! Can't you hear me?!"

They stare. The young age of the girls makes each of the woman's curse words count triple. She feels her naughty language like a painful lash, producing more awful language, the worst words she can imagine. "Cunts! Cunts! Poor people!" She says it, screams it.

Finally one of the girls holds up her hands, gesturing to the mother and the other child. She speaks in sign language, a secret conversation the woman can't understand, and when the girl's done both the mother and the children begin to laugh again so loudly, almost as if they are deaf, almost as if their ears can't judge the level of the laughter they make.

"I hate you! I hate all of you!" the woman screams, and does not stop screaming even after she's back inside, the sliding door slammed shut, her awful reflection the only image in the glass.

OXTR

oxytocin receptor
inducer of uterine contractions during parturition
and of milk ejection, modulator of a variety of
behaviors, including stress and anxiety, social memory
and recognition, sexual and aggressive behaviors,
bonding and maternal behavior

Here's a young nun, a novice at a convent that hasn't been able to entice young women to stay in over twenty years. None except for her. She lives now on a mountain where many of her older sisters are preparing for death, so that one day, when she's done ministering to all their needs, all their last rights, she'll be left alone, the last nun standing. In some small way, she's looking forward to that.

TP53
tumor protein p53
regulates cell division and prevents tumor formation, "guardian of the genome"

A couple rents an upstate cottage beside a river, total luxury. Their dog can run for miles undisturbed. The bottom floor houses a full-size indoor pool where they can swim parallel to the river with the current, against the current, with the current. Escaping all of the river's inconveniences: ice, rain, barges, toxic PCBs.

The house is decorated in Pottery Barn. It is complete. It is blank. The nondescript furniture allows renters to insert their own lives, like the decor of a just-fine business hotel. Everything has been calculated to cause the least upset.

When they arrive, the woman who owns the property greets them. She gives them a quick tour. She shows them linens, garbage disposal, and light switches. Everything is perfect, they tell her.

"Yes. I made sure of it." She smiles. "Here's a phone number should anything crop up."

At first, it is hard for them, city people, to not be busy. They make informal schedules: breakfast, hike, lunch in town, massages, naps, dinner prep, dinner, Netflix, bed, so that it isn't until their second afternoon that one of them shakes off the comfort of the deep couch and says, "You know, I'm going to give that swimming pool a try."

He tops off his prosecco and heads downstairs. He slips into his swimsuit and pulls goggles down over his eyes. Then he removes his swimsuit. Who needs a swimsuit in a private pool? He drains his glass and dips one foot. The water is frigid. What had she said about controlling the temperature? He wishes he'd been listening better, but he was distracted by the pool, the views of the river, the mountains beyond. He dips his foot again. It is too cold for swimming. He'll have to call. No big deal. They paid a lot of money for the rental and so far they've been nothing but perfect, quiet guests. He dials and after three rings gets an answer.

"Hello?" A man.

"Sorry to bother you. This is . . ." and he says his name. "I'm in the rental house this week. Quick question. I'm trying to take a swim and the pool's frigid. Is there some way to make the water warmer?"

Then the question hangs as if the person is slow or old or doesn't understand.

"Hello?"

"The unthinkable has happened." Finally the man speaks.

"Sorry? What's that?"

"Cynthia went to the city, rode an elevator up as high as she could and found a way out. She jumped. She's dead," the man reports.

Later that night the renter finds a thermostat for the pool in the downstairs utility closet. Everything has been calculated to cause the least upset. The feet leaving the ledge. In the morning a friend arrives for a visit. She brings her children. Eventually, the water in the pool warms up. None of them dare to jump in.

PGR

progesterone receptor
associated with the establishment and
maintenance of pregnancy

Her partner had been dead for years when, in her late seventies, she grew interested in Skype. Real space-age stuff to someone born during World War I. Seeing the person on the phone. The woman had learned of Skype from the story of an academic who'd suffered round after round of Skype interviews with college search committees. During the last interview, after she used the words "hegemony" and "transmedia" and "intersectionality" and the search committee still measured disappointment, the academic lifted a pistol from the couch cushions and fired it directly into the tiny flashing camera of her monitor, the secret tunnel to that conference room of scholars with health insurance. She pulled the trigger. She blew those fuckers away.

"What is this Skype?" the older woman asked, and was told. Since then, she's become an expert. Facebook, e-mail, Google, Twitter, Instagram, and now Skype. She spent her life as a photojournalist, traveling the world. Now that she's older she travels less but fills this void by exploring the Internet. She sometimes even photographs her monitor or television set. She snaps Polaroids of celebrity divorces, lurid courtrooms, gossip TV.

Late one night she stumbles across Chatroulette, an online service much like Skype, linking people via video stream. Only, Chatroulette moves randomly from one user to another, linking strangers. More than fostering international dialogues, most Chatroulette conversations start with this: "Show me your tits."

She has nothing to fear from the cock-strokers. They are far away and she is an older, confident woman. When she tires of watching one penis she simply clicks on to the next.

Within moments she's comfortable with the spectacle. The only thing that manages to surprise her is when she comes across someone who really does just want to chat.

She photographs her screen, some graphic images, some more interested in the quality of the light, the line of the object. Night after night she trolls Chatroulette for the better part of an hour looking for life, hearing the same entreaty, "Show me your tits. Show me your tits."

That's a tricky request. She lost her bosom in a double mastectomy years earlier. She never bothered with a reconstruction. It seemed not worth the effort and money, but she recognizes the one-sided nature of her presence on Chatroulette. Getting photographs for free. Giving nothing in return.

One night she lifts her blouse overhead. Her face is hidden while her chest is on display. The double scars of her surgery look like a pair of huge eyes sealed shut forever. The seam of scar tissue. She doesn't like that idea;

still she allows people to look all they want. From beneath her shirt she even recognizes the sound of orgasm once or twice. Eventually the image of the sealed eyelids becomes more than she can bear. "Let me look," she says from beneath her shirt, imagining her scars opening, letting in the light. "Let me look," lowering her blouse, her eyes adjusting to the blinding monitor that's rewired sight all together. "Let me look." One hand on her camera, her eye. "Let me look. Let me look. Let me look."

What is taking Sam so long to come back to bed?

So much time has passed since he left. I shake off the sheets and covers. I call from the top of the stairs. "Sam?" I rest my hand against the window in the hall and hear that awful sound again. A man outside coughing in the night. "Sam?" Each step down the stairs takes years. I'm frozen by terror. How long has Sam been gone? The photos lining the stairwell don't anchor me. Pictures of my girls at birthdays, the beach, soccer games. "Sam?" I call to him from the bottom stair. The front doorknob spins against the lock and I cannot move. I forgot the baseball bat, too. Someone is trying to get inside. There is nothing I can do to stop him, the man who has come to chop us into tiny bits. The lock holds, but I am petrified. The man tries the handle again.

"Sam? Where are you?"

"I'm out here." He spins the locked handle.

"You?" Sam is the man. "How'd you get locked out?" I grab one corner of the kitchen table.

"Are you kidding?" It is Sam at the door. I see him

through the glass, coughing, mortal. Sam's the man who's come to chop us to bits. No wonder I kicked him out. No wonder I changed the locks. If he cannot stop death, what good is he?

"Open the door. Please. I'm so tired," he says.

I look at the night that absorbed my life. How am I supposed to know what's love, what's fear? "If you're Sam who am I?"

"I know who you are."

"You do?"

"Yeah."

"Who?" *Don't say wife*, I think. *Don't say mother*. I put my face to the glass, but it's dark. I don't reflect. Sam and I watch each other through the window of the kitchen door. He coughs some more.

"I want to come home," he says. "I want us to be okay. That's it. Simple. I want to come home and be a family."

"But I am not simple." My body's coursing with secret genes and hormones and proteins. My body made eyeballs and I have no idea how. There's nothing simple about eyeballs. My body made food to feed those eyeballs. How? And how can I not know or understand the things that happen inside my body? That seems very dangerous. There's nothing simple here. I'm ruled by elixirs and compounds. I am a chemistry project conducted by a wild child. I am potentially explosive. Maybe I love Sam because hormones say I need a man to kill the coyotes at night, to bring my babies meat. But I don't want caveman love. I want love that lives outside the body. I want love that lives.

"In what ways are you not simple?"

I think of the women I collected upstairs. They're inside me. And they are only a small fraction of the catalog. I think of molds, of the sea, the biodiversity of plankton. I think of my dad when he was a boy, when he was a tree bud. "It's complicated," I say, and then the things I don't say yet. Words aren't going to be the best way here. How to explain something that's coming into existence?

"I get that now." His shoulders tremble some. They jerk. He coughs. I have infected him.

"Sam." We see each other through the glass. We witness each other. That's something, to be seen by another human, to be seen over all the years. That's something, too. Love plus time. Love that's movable, invisible as a liquid or gas, love that finds a way in. Love that leaks.

"Unlock the door," he says.

"I don't want to love you because I'm scared."

"So you imagine bad things about me. You imagine me doing things I've never done to get rid of me. Kick me out so you won't have to worry about me leaving?"

"Yeah," I say. "Right." And I'm glad he gets that.

Sam cocks his head the same way a coyote might, a coyote who's been temporarily confused by a question of biology versus morality.

What's the difference between living and imagining? What's the difference between love and security? Coyotes are not moral.

"Unlock the door?" he asks.

This family is an experiment, the biggest I've ever been part of, an experiment called: How do you let someone in?

"Unlock the door," he says again. "Please."

I release the lock. I open the door. That's the best definition of love.

Sam comes inside. He turns to shut the door, then stops himself. He stares out into the darkness where he came from. What does he think is out there? What does he know? Or is he scared I'll kick him out again? That *is* scary. "What if we just left the door open?" he asks.

"Open." And more, more things I don't say about the bodies of women.

"Yeah."

"What about skunks?" I mean burglars, gangs, evil.

We both peer out into the dark, looking for these scary things. We watch a long while. The night does nothing.

"We could let them in if they want in," he says, but seems uncertain still.

"Really?"

He draws the door open wider and we leave it that way, looking out at what we can't see. Unguarded, unafraid, love and loved. We keep the door open as if there are no doors, no walls, no skin, no houses, no difference between us and all the things we think of as the night.

WAMPUM

"That's a pretty wheelbarrow." But it isn't a wheelbarrow at all. It's a plain wire cart for hauling groceries, laundry. She's trying to keep to the road's shoulder, but a vehicle would still have to cross the yellow lines to get by. He doesn't pass. He rides just behind.

Her walk, slowed by the heat, changes his breath. She tightens her ponytail and he readjusts his hands on the steering wheel. She scratches a bug bite on the back of her leg and he offers her a ride. Either he'll chop her up into body parts or he'll drop her off at her house. "Thank you," she says. "I'd love a ride. It's hot out here."

Trey throws her cart into the backseat. His dashboard is burgundy plastic. It smells like it's melting. He wears a piece of string around his wrist and says little. The radio is playing "Oh, won't you, show me the way?" That old song. She doesn't even know how old, but long before she was born. The closer they get to her house the more she thinks he might drive past it and she'll be as good as gone.

But he's got more structured plans. He pulls into her driveway. "If there's anything you ever need."

"There might be," she tells him. "What's your name? Just in case."

"Trey."

She was only asking to be coy. She's known his name since she was nine years old.

There's nothing to do in the summertime. Sit on the porch. Hang laundry on the line. Sometimes she goes to a 4-H meeting, though she has no luck keeping chickens. They don't like her. They don't lay eggs. She gets her period, feels sick for a day and stays home watching TV. There's a party in town on the Fourth of July, but not if it rains. There's a parish fair in August and a pageant that celebrates the Europeans who bought this town from the Indians for a couple of beads, some shiny coins, and a rifle. That's how the summer passes. That and an occasional night of baby-sitting at four dollars an hour, country wages, no-driver's-license wages.

She walks to the store. She can't get her driver's license yet, and even then she won't have a car. She buys candy in town and it feels like she's gotten something accomplished. She's walking home, eating a Tootsie Pop, when Trey pulls up beside her for the second time. One action means something to her and something entirely different to him.

"Where's your wheelbarrow?"

With a fingernail she dislodges the candy glommed onto her teeth. "I didn't need it today."

"So you just left it at home."

"That's right."

Stupid stuff, like he's speaking in code. "Wheelbarrow" stands for something else he can't say. But how is she supposed to know that?

"It's a hot one."

"Yes, it is." Heat waves rise off the road up ahead.

"You have any interest in heading down to the quarry for a swim?"

"I don't have a bathing suit on."

His stomach sours because now he absolutely, definitely has thought of this young girl standing before him naked.

"I could stop at home and grab one."

"All right."

"Wait here though. My mother didn't like your car the other day."

At the quarry Trey pulls off his shirt. He wears a pair of running shorts the same color as his car. They are cut higher than the surfer trunks boys her age prefer. Trey's shorts are the kind that sometimes accidentally expose a man. The first time she ever caught a glimpse was one of her mother's boyfriends in a pair of running shorts. She thought there was something wrong with him. What she saw looked tortured and red, wrinkled as a turkey's snood.

Trey's hands are ruddy from working. That triggers a feeling inside, like she can see him using those hands to battle a woolly mammoth, drag it home for her supper. He has hair on his chest, at least one curl for every year he's been alive. Thirty-six, thirty-seven, thirty-eight. She can't count them all. He dives into the quarry with his baseball cap still on his head, hiding something underneath.

They are trespassing, but all the kids do it. All the kids and Trey. Below the surface of the water there are broken beer bottles, brown shards coated with scum.

"Come here, little mouse."

The words he uses. She slouches her back and stares down at him from the rocks. He has tufts of dark hair on his knuckles. A few longer mustache whiskers poke into his mouth. Trey has a mustache. She dives into the quarry after him.

Since she was seven she's kept a white pocketbook filled with special things, a treasure purse. There's a Kennedy half-dollar and a stick with a worm pattern eaten into it. There's a small rubber monster for the end of a pencil. There's a half-gone pack of Merit cigarettes. She found some of the treasure along the road into town, things that had flown out of people's open car windows as they went speeding past. Some of the treasure came from a burned-down house. Some of the treasure is stones with bits of mica inside. Once, she found a blue Mylar balloon that had lost its air. She took it home. She put it with the other treasures. There is a piece of fake tiger skin in the purse. There are some seashells and old acorns and a tiny plastic bull another boyfriend of her mom's brought back from Spain, where he was stationed. When she spreads this collection on her bed it feels like she owns lots of things: she's rich. Her mother says, "Why do you hold on to all this junk?" But then her mom will finger a rusted thimble or a rubber-band ball. The purse makes the girl happy, the same way she used to feel after baking mud pies all afternoon. She'd made something of value from nothing and all she had to do was wait for the right person to come along and ask for it. "Two mud pies? That will be three stones with flecks of mica in them. Thank you."

At first, everything Trey touched went into the treasure purse, even if it was just a pen or a lighter. But then he started touching too many things and she had to become more selective.

Her mother's not very religious. Her mother went to college. Still, someone convinced her to join a group going on a three-day Christian retreat. A weekend up by Winamac Lake, three and a half hours away. Her mom thinks maybe she'll meet a nice man. "A new father for you," she says. The girl's already had two new fathers plus the original one. Her mother registered for the retreat and they sent a brochure. *Brothers and Sisters*, it said. *Today, perhaps more than ever, it is necessary to remind ourselves that without God we are nothing, bereft of value, incapable of doing anything.* Her mother decided to go anyway. For three days.

"I really need to get away." She plays with her daughter's hair. Her bag is packed. "You'll understand when you're older." Which is a sticking point between them. The girl already thinks she is older. After all, she's not going to get any taller than this. After all, her mother is about to leave her home alone for three days.

"I've got to get away, baby. Be with some people my age, you know? I mean, I really, really need this." Her mother smiles beautifully. The girl doesn't doubt that what she says is true, but there are things the girl really, really needs also. Still, she tries to act like an adult. Her mother doesn't belong to her. Her mother needs this.

The car pulls out of the driveway and, left alone, the girl creeps through the house. It's so quiet that even sitting on the sofa makes a huge noise. She moves like light, silent but not unnoticed through the hallway, into the dining room they never use, out back into the yard. No one is there.

It isn't until much later that she starts to feel scared, once it seems certain that the sun will set and she will be alone until day breaks again. That changes everything. She locks the doors, but that does nothing to keep the darkness out. There are gaps, secret holes in the house. There are bushes right outside where anything could hide. The kitchen cabinets look sinister. She doesn't open them. She turns on the TV in the living room to have a voice nearby. That way, if she hears something like a floorboard creaking upstairs or a man sharpening his butcher knife she can blame it on the TV even if she knows it's not the TV.

In the morning she's happy to find that she survived the night, but she's not going to take any chances again. She picks up the phone.

"Remember you said if I ever needed anything?"

"Sort of." Trey exhales, the breath amplified by the telephone line.

"You said it."

"Okay. All right."

"Well. Do you want to come over for supper tonight? I'll cook it for you."

"You want to make me dinner?"

"Sure."

"What about your mother?"

"She's out of town."

There is a lot of silence on the line—space for her to imagine the room he's standing in. Torn linoleum and a kitchen table painted to look like oak. Dog hair everywhere. A chipped china sugar bowl someone she doesn't know anything about once gave Trey.

"What time?" he asks.

Her mother left her with plenty to eat: cottage cheese, sliced salami, some frozen dumplings, canned soup, peas. Nothing she could serve a man for dinner. She has twenty dollars, emergency money. When she hangs up the phone with Trey she's all air. That seems like an emergency to her.

At the store she purchases chicken breasts, broccoli, white rice, and frozen pound cake. She waits outside for a guy who agrees to buy her wine coolers. He says it's no trouble at all and starts to laugh. He enjoys holding that door open for her.

"Ding dong," Trey says. Her or the sound a doorbell would make?

"Trey," and then properly, "Won't you please come in?"

She's conscious of where he looks, though there's nothing unusual about her house: overstuffed, windows that have slipped some from their sills, dusty rugs, and on the walls, prints of fishermen in dangerous waters.

"I've got to finish up in the kitchen." And into the kitchen they both go. She takes the broccoli off the stove and pours it through a colander. The steam rises up around her head and Trey, as if blown by the wind, presses his body up against her back. *There*, she thinks, *now, finally, he will kill me.* He grabs on to the edge of the sink and pulls in tightly, holding on, spooning her from behind. She stills the colander. He moves his hands up to her neck. No one says a thing. He breathes behind her ear, covering and calming her the way one might an epileptic. Which is close to what she feels like.

Trey was in his twenties the day she was born. She doesn't fight him off. She wants to see just how wrong something can get.

Eventually he clears his throat. He lets her go. The wind dies down and Trey has a seat.

It turns out not to matter much what she made for dinner. Trey stares at her while he eats, not noticing the difference: broccoli, chicken, rice. She wishes they could agree not to talk, better to just sit there looking at each other, but she can't keep her mouth from moving.

"You all right?" she asks him when the room gets too quiet.

"Fine, fine, fine." He doesn't want his wine cooler. She drinks two and pours him a glass of milk for dinner. She eats slowly. She's not sure how things are going to go afterward and she wants time to make a plan.

"Down in Florida," he says finally, "some people went out on their motorboat for a joyride. When they couldn't see land anymore they stopped for a swim. One, two, three, four they jumped overboard, cannonballing, back dives from the deck, showing off. They swam about, joking, talking about the food they were going to eat, the beers they were going to drink that afternoon. Eventually one woman got cold and headed back to the boat. That was when they realized their trouble. No one had let down a ladder. At first it was funny. They were bobbing a few feet away from their potato salad, their cell phones, and not one of them could scale the side of that fiberglass boat." Trey strokes his chin to make her wait for the rest of the story. "The Coast Guard found the boat a couple days later, floating like a phantom ship. Hamburgers and whatnot, rotted in the sun, covered with flies. The bodies washed up later."

The girl wonders if Trey planned to tell her this story. If he'd saved up something to talk about, something he thought might make her like him, a story about dead people and flies. She feels sorry for Trey. He doesn't understand much.

"They found a lady's fingernail dug into the side of the boat." Trey raises his eyebrows for her reaction.

"How'd you know what kind of dives and jumps they did if no one lived?"

He looks off over her head and laughs before taking a bite of food. He chews slowly, swallows. "Isn't that it exactly?" He snaps his lips together. "That's the difference between where you're at and where I'm standing."

"What?"

"You've got a clearer view."

"Well, you've got your driver's license."

No plan comes to her and the meal is done. Trey wipes his mouth on a napkin before standing up. She doesn't look at him. She knows he's coming.

When he kisses her she has a strange thought: *I'm kissing a water buffalo or maybe a rhinoceros, a creature foreign and large, an animal only seen in photos.* Maybe it's his mustache. He grabs on to her butt with both hands kneading and dividing. Strange new territory, and all she wonders is *What's next? What is the next thing he'll do to me?* And then, *Do it now,* because she needs to know what comes next.

Each move he makes gets carved into her. Not her flesh, as flesh heals, but carved like stone. She'll have his sharpness and breath with her always now. She'll be an old woman sitting on a porch and she'll be able to pull Trey out, get that moment back whenever she needs it, even if he's dead then.

Trey lifts up her shirt. Puts his mouth there. Alien blossoms, Martian fungus, her chest. She watches the top of his head, his hairs boring secret tunnels into his skull. They lie down on the couch and his weight doesn't crush her. He fits there. He presses through her jeans over and again. Something strange that she likes. She closes her eyes. Up ahead is a gate. Trey knows the way, knows the guards, and they are almost through, but Trey stops. He stills himself, rigid like he's heard a person calling his name.

The gate slams shut. She's back in her living room, eyes wide open, fourteen years old.

Their damp skin sticks together. "Here's to old Kentucky," he says.

She has no idea what that means. They don't live anywhere near Kentucky. A car passes on the road and it sounds like everyone who stayed young is out having a good time. Fine. Let them go.

She doesn't know whether or not Trey and she did it. Her pants are still on. She thinks that means no, but there's a lot she's unsure of and would feel foolish to ask, embarrassed to learn she'd left the deed undone, like a little girl. "You want to see something?" she asks.

Trey sits up, releasing her. It takes him a while to answer, staring through the small window over her mother's chair, wincing. The first stars are coming out and Trey's communing with them. "Well," he says, as if making a really tough decision.

"It's no big deal," she says. "Hold on."

"All right." Trey rakes his fingers across the thighs of his jeans.

For one moment upstairs, hands on the purse, she thinks this might be a bad idea.

She pushes their dinner plates off to the side of the table. "Come here."

"What have we got?" Trey asks, genuinely surprised.

"Treasure." She unzips the bag and dumps the contents out onto the kitchen table.

Trey's eyes move from a hunk of quartz to a pencil nub, from her Mexican postage stamp to a small bead with a peace sign carved into it. "What have we got?" he asks again, barely breaking a whisper. His jaw firm with disbelief. He fingers some of the objects: a few wildflowers pressed between wax paper, a dead bumblebee in a magnifying box. "Treasure?"

"I've had it since I was young."

"Since you were young." He picks up a tiny, empty bottle of perfume that makes his hands look giant. The night starts to tick. Trey lifts a button of red glass, then puts it down. "I'm going to ask you something and I think I want you to tell me the truth."

"All right."

"How old are you?"

She draws her index finger across her neck where a heat is rising. Trey has cracked open. This question makes her angry. "Let me sit on your lap," she commands.

He presses his thumbs hard into the corners of his eyes before shoving back from the table to make room. She takes a seat on one of his knees, trying to be light. "Shit," he says. They look at the treasure spread before them.

"I'm fourteen and you already knew that." A lens cap without a camera. An old retractable pen that says CHAMPION on it. "I found this on Brannah Street." She's being nice, trying to stop him from ruining everything. "And this I pulled off a chair my mother was getting rid of." She passes him a brass upholstery tack.

Trey's face tightens. He doesn't deny knowing her age, but the lie he'd told himself about fourteen has dissolved. Fourteen is a girl.

Back in high school things had been going so well for him. She watches him finger a pull-top beer tab, a bit of coal, a scratch-n-sniff sticker, a small golden bell. Then he sees it. He lifts it from the pile. YUMA TRACK, it says on a pink cigarette lighter she's stolen from him.

"What's this doing here?"

The miniature head of a Japanese doll. A boll of cotton. And that lighter, because Trey is treasure to her.

"Let me keep it." She turns her body toward his. "I'll trade you."

Trey spins his lighter head over tail, head over tail. "Oh." He pulls back from what he'd started. "That'd be a very bad trade on your part." She can hear him breathing, slipping away. "No." His leg is unforgiving and every bit of strength she had over him vanishes, a switch clicking off.

They sit there a long while in the quiet until she finds the thing she's looking for: What would happen to him if she called the cops? It's a funny question, interesting. It makes her smile, so she rubs her face to hide the grin. He'd learn how old fourteen is.

"I've got to go." Trey slides her off his lap like she has cooties. Fine. If she has cooties, she got them from him. What would he do if she called the cops? She studies the kitchen linoleum.

"Bye." Just on his breath. "See you," he says.

"When?" Breath sours swiftly. She rolls onto the sides of her feet. The night keeps swinging, Trey to her, Trey to her.

"I don't know. Sometime. You all right?" he asks.

"Sure."

And then he tries to hand her two twenties. She can smell him. She doesn't take the money.

"What?"

She stares a hole in his chest. "This is all I've got," she says, knowing it's not true. Knowing that when she looks to her treasures, Trey's lighter will still be there along with his finger bone, maybe his sternum, his kneecap, his lips and lungs, even that lady's torn-off fingernail, and later, after he's gone, she'll pack them all back up into her purse.

Sometimes it can take years and years to say who got the better end of a deal. Who made out like a bandit. Her mother or God. The Europeans or the Indians. Trey or her. The people on that boat or the ocean. Maybe, she thinks, something really, really awful had just been about to happen to those people and they avoided it by drowning instead. Though of course it's hard to think of something worse than clawing for your life in the middle of the ocean.

The phone is on the wall. It would be so easy to describe his car to the cops. Her mother might see the blue lights flashing all the way up in Winamac Lake. Maybe even her dads would see the lights.

She makes tight fists, hoping to steer the night. *Come closer*, she thinks, but Trey walks from the room. He swears quietly in the hall. *Closer.* The cops and the phone wait. The front door latches behind Trey on his way out, and night comes down around her older and colder than it's ever been before.

THE STORY OF OF

In a coffee shop on Dead Elm Street, Norma rearranges chicken bones on her plate, making an arrow that points at her stomach, where the chicken's meat now resides. She'd once seen a picture of a hen in a science book. Remember? The hen had been split open down the breast, unzipped like a parka. Inside was a chain of eggs, rubbery as tapioca, small getting smaller. Nothing like the basket of fried chicken Norma has just finished eating, but sickening. Yes, sickening, a ride going round and round. You can't make it stop.

Norma's husband's brother's wife, Damica, sits across the table bouncing The Baby on her knee. Outside, automobiles are stopping at the stop sign. Some go left, some keep right on going.

Damica's talking. "If it's all the same to you I'll—"

"It's never all the same," Norma says, thinking of the chain of eggs. "It changes a tiny bit every time."

But Damica keeps talking. "—I'll just get your lunch tomorrow, 'cause all I have is a twenty."

Dead Elm Street is not a dead-end street. Hand on a butter knife, Norma cuts the street in half. Procreation by division, just like the amoebae.

The waitress stops by the table. "You girls need anything else?"

"No," Damica says. "Just the check."

"Do you have any walnuts?" Norma asks.

"Walnuts?"

"Walnuts," Norma confirms.

"No," the waitress answers. "No walnuts, no pecans, no filberts. No nuts."

"Walnuts?" Damica asks.

"They get you pregnant."

"Walnuts get you pregnant?"

"I read it on the Internet."

Damica curls her mouth into a half-smile like she's saying, *I doubt it*. Damica is very pretty, part Dutch, part Puerto Rican, but all of her good looks didn't make her a genius, so Norma wonders what the hell Damica might know about the health benefits of walnuts. Nothing, she decides. Nothing.

The Baby burps. Damica plants some Eskimo kisses on her newborn's nose. The Baby does not have a name yet, and its namelessness makes The Baby seem larger than it is, like a hairless, diapered buffalo on her sister-in-law's lap, having a sip of formula.

They can't decide and, rather than narrowing, the list of possible baby names grows each day. Part of the problem is that her husband's brother, Scott—or his name used to be Scott before he changed it to Rider—is very creative. Highlights from the list of names include: Potemkin, Shade, Marble, Electric, Trouble, America, Nautica, Chrysanthemum, Fraction, Frame, and Plaid.

"Nautica?" Norma asked.

"Rider says it means ocean."

Norma thinks it just means sportswear.

Norma and Damica eat lunch together nearly every day, so they don't always have to talk. They are used to each other the way people are used to their TV sets. The hum keeps them warm even if they aren't listening to the broadcast.

Damica was once Damica LaMotteo, but now she and Norma, having married brothers, have the same last name, far less beautiful than LaMotteo. Norma and Damica Jonsen. Plain, but it presents a united front like a uniform Norma puts on every morning, and since Norma has recently lost her job, a uniform feels all right.

Norma enjoys these lunches. If she weren't here, she'd be glued to her computer, reading posts on Trying to Conceive (TTC) chat rooms.

> **baby37**: thanks to clomid I tried to shove my husband down the stairs yesterday.
>
> **infertilems.**: just found out health insurance won't pay for my three $15,000 IVFs that didn't work
>
> **wannabb**: implantation bleeding? anyone?
>
> **baby37**: implantation bleeding is a myth spread by women who have no trouble conceiving. there's no such thing, wannabb. that's your period

whynotme: had one HSG, one D&C and am now
  using both OPK and BBT while TTC. Any
  advice?

Norma hasn't had any tests. She's never even spoken to her
doctor about what is wrong. She knows what's wrong, or at
least she thinks she knows what's wrong, why she can't
have a baby of her own, and it isn't something she wants to
talk to her doctor about. "Ted's cheating on me."

The Baby sits up quickly and draws its eyes wide open,
staring across the table at Norma, surprised, the way sleeping cats realize they need to be somewhere else and dash
out of a room. The Baby stares at Norma. Norma stares
back. All it takes to make a pair of eyeballs is a mother and
a father. No Japanese porcelain facility, no Silicon Valley
tech lab.

"Oh, come on, Norm. Not this again. Come on." Norma
brings up the topic of Ted's alleged cheating a lot.

"Why not? Because I have no proof? That doesn't mean
he's not."

Ted works all the time. He says he has to, to make the
payments on their mortgage, but Norma didn't even want
the stupid mortgage in the first place. Ted recognized a role
and started playing it. A few summers back he convinced
Norma that they should move into a new development
called Rancho de Caza. "Temporarily," he said. "We won't
spend our whole life living in a development."

When they moved in, Rancho de Caza was not a gated
community. Norma insisted on that. But then the burglaries started and after a thirty-eight-year-old mother from

Lilac Lane was lashed to a kitchen chair with duct tape and thrown into her belowground swimming pool, the board of Rancho de Caza changed their minds. Even though the woman lived.

Now when Norma walks home she must stand in front of the guardhouse, wave to the man inside, and then wait while he swings open the wrought-iron gates, big enough for an eighteen-wheeler. Norma, tiny and weak as a mouse, scurries down Day Lily.

Norma pulls today's paper from her purse. Bypassing the front page's headlines, she flips to page eleven, where her favorite column appears. The local political beat—town hall, zoning boards, Department of Waste Management–type concerns. Lately, Harrison Nembridge, reporter-at-large, has been following a trademark case. Nembridge's stories are poorly written, full of attendance rosters and incomprehensibly dry legal terms. Still, Norma's hooked because the case has universal ramifications in a way very few things in her small city do.

The plaintiff is a man named Drake, a onetime lawyer who'd caught the entrepreneurial spirit three years ago when, in his spare time, he began trademarking words from the English language, claiming them for his own use within a certain-mile radius of Norma's city. He chose simple words like "best" or "with" or, his money maker, "the." Drake's represented by the lawyer Linda Kanakas. Linda was two classes ahead of Norma in grade school and Linda was a tough one. The sort of girl everyone knew. Linda was a bully, and while it hasn't been proven, there was a rumor that when Linda was in junior high she called Immigration Services to report an undocumented man, Hector Donoso. Hector's daughter, Mary, was dating a debate team star Linda had her eye on. Hector was deported back to Honduras. Mary and her mother had to move into Section 8 housing in another district.

The defendant in the Drake copyright case is Marguerite Eddell, Jim Eddell's widow. Eddell now owns her dead husband's auto parts store, House of Mufflers. Linda and Drake are suing Eddell for the unattributed use of the word "of" in all company materials and advertising.

"I have to go," Damica says. "Will you hold The Baby for a second?"

Norma looks over the edge of the paper. "Yeah. Sure. Just let me pee." She folds the newspaper.

The stalls of the ladies' room are made of cool aluminum. Norma rests her head against this coolness while she pees. In the stall wall she can see a distorted reflection. The dark chestnut hair dye she tried last month looks black, and her now black hair, against her pale skin, makes every minor bump and blemish on her face red and raw as if she'd been picking at the imperfections.

Norma is thinking about Damica's twenty-dollar bill. Norma is wondering why her sister-in-law never pays for lunch. Then Norma feels something peeling away. A streamer of blood sinks to the bottom of the toilet bowl, a dark, dead fish.

When Norma once asked Damica how long it took her to get pregnant, Damica said, "I don't know. How long does it take? Fifteen minutes?" So Norma said, "No. I mean, how many times did you have to try?" And Damica said, "Try? What do you mean, honey?"

Norma and Ted have been trying for over two years. Each time Norma gets her period, strength leaks out of her. Iron and blood. Sex feels like death.

She can hardly blame Ted for finding a girlfriend. Maybe she should look for a boyfriend. Maybe he could get her pregnant. Maybe none of this matters at all—love, babies, marriage.

She rests her forehead on the aluminum. She pokes her belly sharply. "Wake up." She speaks to her ovaries, imagining them as something crinkled and squished, like the wicked witch's feet underneath the tornado house. GIVE ME A CALL. 1-800-FUCKIN'A is scratched into the bathroom wall. Still seated on the toilet, Norma digs her cell phone out from the bottom of her purse. She dials.

"Hello?"

"Hi. 1-800-FUCKIN'A?"

"No, I'm sorry. You've reached 1-800-DUBL-INC. Doubles Incorporated, providing goods and services for the Procreation by Division Industries."

"Procreation by division?"

"Yeah. You know, like the amoebae."

Norma hangs up quickly.

Norma pays for Damica's lunch and on her walk home she takes a left off Dead Elm Street onto Larre Road, pronounced "Larry." Norma presses her fingers hard into the corners of her eyes. Crying is something she started doing after the first year of trying to have a baby. Now she is really good at crying. She doesn't even have to practice in front of the mirror anymore. Larre Road is a great place to cry, as very few people come this way.

Her city allowed for generous strips of grass between the sidewalks and the street. These greenways are mandatorily maintained by the business or homeowner who lives nearby. They have in the past been canvases for competing civic landscaping pride. But down here on Larre Road there are no businesses. There are old farms and fallow fields. The sidewalks make reverse mohawks through tall yellow grass high as Norma's waist. If a car were to drive past, Norma would appear to be swimming in a sea of yellow and green. That is, if Norma didn't duck down and hide in the grass each time a car approached.

Norma no longer owns a car because no one told her to change the oil. They kept that information a big secret and she ruined the engine of the used Ford Escort Ted had bought her. She blew the head gasket. Now she can't stand people who have cars that work. Everyone has a baby and everyone drives a car with perfectly functioning air conditioners. No one has their windows rolled down. They want to make sure their babies are comfortable in their air-conditioned car seats.

A little killing bit each day.

Shutting off one nostril at a time, Norma blows her nose into the grass. Then her crying is over for today.

Larre Road is not a direct route home, but it is quiet and golden for now. The housing developments haven't moved in here yet, though telltale plastic orange surveyor's ribbons dot the way. They'll be here soon. In recent years the city has been spreading out, grabbing land like a desperate hand sinking in quicksand, trying to take all the ground down with it. Soon there will be nothing left that is unknowable, unlit, and mysterious. There will be no more of the dark dark.

Today Larre Road is deserted and sunny. It is warm and peaceful. It reminds Norma of junior high, after lunch. She'd return to her classroom to find that the afternoon activity included a filmstrip. "Digestion and You," or "Mammals!" As the teacher dimmed the lights Norma would slip into a trance that wasn't sleep but borrowed from sleep's best aspects, like being able to fly or make out with the kid seated behind you, and no one else in class would see your young bodies writhing together underneath the desks in a mass of sixth-grade flesh. Larre Road is a secret tunnel back to a land of peaceful, warm sixth-grade afternoons. Norma can almost hear someone saying, "Psst. C'mon. This way." And into the tunnel she goes.

A rustling speeds up behind her quickly. From around the bend in the sidewalk comes a woman riding a boy's BMX bike. The woman's age is hard to guess. Her face is sharp. The blades of her cheekbones could cut, as they've been accentuated by two brutish swaths of rouge, leaving sallow caverns around her mouth. The woman wears her hair feathered back with a rolled bandana across her forehead. Olivia Newton John, let's get physical. The woman looks tough, dirty, and perhaps a bit deformed. Her eyes are watery and distracted as a drug addict's. Her body is disconcertingly tiny, like a ten-year-old body has been grafted onto a forty-year-old head.

Norma doesn't know this woman so she thinks prostitute, no, drug dealer. No, prostitute.

They are the only two people on Larre Road but the woman stares straight ahead as if Norma weren't there at all. The woman clenches a cigarette between her lips, one hand on the handlebars, one hand dangling by her side. She doesn't blink, and in a fast breeze she glides past Norma and is gone.

Creepy, Norma thinks, but creepy like a humongous pile of insects crawling on top of one another, a pile of insects Norma would want to poke from afar with a long stick.

Larre Road changes from meadow to pine forest. The air turns damp and the sidewalk is darker with moss. The sky is blocked by pine boughs that keep her best thoughts from escaping up into the atmosphere. She follows Larre Road up to the driveway of the old hospital. It's been closed for twenty years. When she was a kid, she'd heard it was haunted. The hospital sits like a gray frog on top of a small hill. Its windows are fenced by wrought iron. It was built as a mansion in 1927 by the explorer Dirmuid Grady, after a trip through the Sangla Valley, where Grady and his party had been looking for Shangri-la, the forbidden and fictional city. Of the twenty-seven people in Grady's outfit, five returned alive. The others had been picked off by illnesses and accidents as if they were a dish of hard candies God was enjoying one by one.

Grady built this gray frog of a house and lived in it for seven months before he himself tripped on an unsecured flagstone, tumbled into the empty concrete swimming pool, and landed in the deep end.

The state bought the mansion for nothing and turned it into a hospital for troubled minds. When Norma was thirteen, the last doctor presided over the last troubled mind, a man named Walter, who confessed he wasn't actually troubled but had come to the sanitarium because he was lonely. The doctor proposed that the two of them should enter retirement together somewhere in the tropics. Walter, the patient, agreed. Page eleven reported the story.

Norma scuffles up to the Institute, unsure if it's trespassing.

A BMX bicycle with fluorescent-green tires has been deposited in the grass by the front door. One wheel spins slowly in the breeze. The warm afternoon. Larre Road feels intimate like a password whispered down a phone line made from two paper cups and a piece of string. Norma thinks, *That terrifying toadish mouse of a woman is waiting inside. Maybe she has come to meet her married boyfriend.* This derangement of the mind is something that happens to women whose husbands cheat on them: the world begins to overflow with people, animals, aunts and uncles all having sex. Everywhere, fucking is going on. The world is an algae-covered pond in spring and Norma alone is standing on the dry bank.

Through a narrow pane of glass by the front door, she sees the tile's been ripped up in a few spots. Water has stained the wallpaper brown but it doesn't look too scary inside. There's sunlight and debris that is nearly modern, an ashtray, a clunky remote control, a pair of Naugahyde chairs. A chain that once secured the doors closed dangles in the breeze.

Norma slips inside. "Hello?"

No one answers.

The air in the sanitarium is holding on to winter. Norma backs herself up against the foyer wall, standing very still, like a moth against mottled bark, blending in. Her eyeballs beat left, right, left, right. She calls again, "Hello?"

No one answers.

The house smells foul, a mouth of rotten teeth. The air's not been stirred in a long time and whatever's in the base-ment (dead bodies, raccoon poop) lingers. Most furnishings have been stolen or damaged by bad kids throwing parties in the old house. They wrote their names, the devil's names, their sweethearts' names on the walls. They peed in the cor-ners, liberated the fire axe from its glass box and splintered a large reception desk with it. One wall has a chair stick-ing straight out of it, all four legs reamed into the plaster. Still, there are remnants of a former glory. Ornate moldings whose details hold hope for a better future, eight different colors of Italian marble, and a mantel raised on the back of a carved oak deer. Norma wonders how long it took to build such a house. A long time.

The central staircase twists smoothly. "Hello?" she calls again, but there is no answer. Many of the banister's sup-ports have been kicked free. From the landing she can see out the back window to what must have once been the pool. After an accident involving some schoolgirls, the town filled the hole with dirt, leaving a square cement corona.

Upstairs she looks left and right. The wings are identical hallways filled with doors. Norma goes right.

"Hello?" she says, nervous now. She glances behind herself, then up. Directly above her the ceiling is stained. A large brown mass of dripping discoloration has spread out in uneven rings. There must be a leak. She circles below, neck craned backward, arms linked across her chest. She's mesmerized, as though the blob were telling her the long secrets of such a stain, thirty-six years of leaking into a mark as dark and deep as this one. Thirty-six years is exactly as long as Norma has been alive. No wonder she feels so empty. Norma exhales. Norma rights her head. And there she is. Standing no more than a narrow foot away. The prostitute/drug dealer stares at Norma as if she is hungry.

"Hello," Norma says.

"What are you doing?"

"Not much."

This woman is filthy. Tiny capillary lines of sweaty grit swoop across her neck, following the contours there. Her fingernails are rimmed with dirt, as if she crawled out of a dug grave. A dark mole on the woman's collarbone is so large it could be the mother ship to all this dirt. Norma feels a shiver. There's power to this woman's filth, a strength in knowing there's nowhere further one can fall.

"What's your name?" the woman asks.

"Norma," Norma says. "What's yours?"

"Norma," the dirty woman answers.

"No really."

"Really. It is."

Norma does not believe her.

"Why are you here?" Dirty Norma asks.

"I don't know."

"They don't accept crazies here anymore, you know."

"What?" Norma asks.

"That's what this place once used to be. A place for crazy people. In each of the rooms." She points down the hall. "Behind each one of these doors doctors used to sit with clipboards asking each and every patient, 'So what's the problem?' and the patients would start again at the beginning, telling the same stories over and over. How they were abused by their fathers or how they were forced to raise monkeys for laboratory testing or how they saw the first atomic bombs blow up in the New Mexico desert or whatever it was that haunted them. Day in and day out the patients would sit in these rooms and tell their stories again and again, and sure, it might change a little each time, until finally the patients realized, after years of talking, that they were fucked and there wasn't much they could do about it.

"That's how it works. Everybody knows that. Don't you know that? You tell the doctor the same story over and over and then one day you realize that the story has changed, and that the new story, well, that's your real problem."

Norma doesn't know what to say. "Behind each one of these doors?"

"Yup," Dirty Norma says. She starts to walk down the hallway. Norma hesitates for a moment and then quickly follows. The patients' rooms are small, and many of the metal-frame beds are still there. In the door of the first room Dirty Norma says, "Look," and points to a murderously filthy mattress. "That's where the kids come to do it now. I've seen them."

Clean Norma studies the mattress.

Dirty Norma watches her. "What? Do you think you're better than them? Better than me?" Her question's not entirely out of the blue. In fact, Norma had just been thinking, *I am better than Dirty Norma. I bet she sleeps on that dirty mattress.*

Though she tries not to, in a whisper Norma answers, "Yes."

"Hmm. Well, you're not. And I can prove it."

"Fine. Prove it."

"We'll have a contest."

"Okay."

"We'll see who knows more."

"Okay," Norma says, though recently she has been allergic to knowledge. She feels that people, her husband, Ted, in particular, with the hefty stack of biographies and histories he keeps piling beside their bed, collect knowledge in the same way that people go shopping and buy a year's supply of antibacterial soap, paper towels, wedding presents, fake ficus trees. Just to have, just in case. Norma's more interested in intuition. Still, she agrees to the contest, certain she knows more than Dirty Norma.

"To start, I know who your husband is sleeping with," Dirty Norma says.

"Who?"

"I'm not just going to just tell you. You have to trade. You have to tell me something I don't know."

"Oh," Norma says, and despite herself, has a seat on the filthy mattress to think. She's tired. "Okay." *What do I know*, she wonders. She has to think for a very long time. What *does* she know? "I know how to make a hot artichoke dip," Norma says.

"Everybody knows that, cup of mayo, cup of cream cheese, cup of canned artichokes, diced."

That was Norma's recipe exactly. "Plus a little garlic," she says, and Dirty Norma just stares without answering, as if the garlic were an unspoken and unimpressive addition. "All right. I know how to recite all the presidents of the United States in order of their presidency."

"Okay. Let's hear it."

"Washington, Adams, Jefferson, Madison, Monroe, Jackson, Van Bur—"

"ERRRRG! Wrong," Dirty Norma calls out. "You messed up. It's Monroe, ADAMS, Jackson. You forgot the second Adams."

And Norma knows Dirty Norma is right. "Fine."

What does Norma know? Not much. She has no knowledge to trade. Nothing. "Come on, just tell me. He's MY husband," she says.

"He's YOURS? Like you own him?"

Norma mulls this over, rolling her head back and forth in her hands. "Yes," she finally decides.

"You OWN him?"

Norma knows it isn't right, but she says it anyway. "Yes. I do."

"Well, even so, you'll have to guess who he's sleeping with, and even if you do guess, I'm not saying I'm going to tell you if you're right or wrong. I just want to see if you can guess."

"Damica," Norma guesses.

"I'm not saying one way or another."

"Look, I don't really care. I'm not even sure if I love him anymore."

"Guess!"

"So it's not Damica?"

"No. But wouldn't that be evil if it were?"

Norma glances around the room. She adjusts her seat up on the bed. Dirty Norma sits down beside her so that their legs are touching and Norma can feel the warmth of her.

"I don't know who," she says.

"I know. You don't know anything and yet you think you're better than me."

Norma stays silent, staring down at an old suitcase left behind in the room, maybe by one of the patients.

"Guess." Dirty Norma stomps her foot like a horse.

"I don't know."

"Fine. I'll tell you. It's Linda Kanakas, you know, the lawyer?"

"Yeah. I know her," Norma says. She's not surprised.

"Finally. You know something. Your husband is sleeping with Linda Kanakas."

It feels good to finally know the truth. But then, in a second or two, it starts to feel really, really bad. Her eyes blur their focus onto the suitcase at her feet. It is a small leather one, an older model, a hard-shell brown Samsonite with a leather edge, probably from the 1940s. Just below the handle on the case is a simple golden latch and a monogram that is all but rubbed off, erasing its owner. Dirty Norma sees Norma looking at it. Thumbing the square of brass, Dirty Norma slides the catch to the left and pops the suitcase's lock. The inside is lined with a forgotten pink taffeta, and the elastic of its side pockets has been stretched into an overextended deformity like a tired and spent girdle. The air inside the case smells yellow and aged. Resting inside is a stenographer's notebook. It must have belonged to one of the patients.

"Let me see." Norma kicks the case so she can look inside. Her grandmother had been a stenographer for forty-seven years, an expert in both Pitman and Gregg shorthand. "That's a stenographer's notebook," Norma says, demonstrating her knowledge.

"Yeah," Dirty Norma says, unimpressed. "It says so right on the cover."

"That doesn't matter. Even if it didn't say it, I would have known." The wire coil across the top, the long, narrow pages divided into two columns. She thinks she might even be able to read some of the shorthand inside and she is certain that Dirty Norma can't read shorthand, but as she picks the notebook up and opens the pad to its first page she finds its contents have not been recorded in the scribble of shorthand but are instead written in plain English.

And so both Normas start to read from the stenographer's pad.

In the coffee shop off Dead Elm Street Norma pushes what's left of her meat loaf aside.

That's what it says in the stenographer's notebook. They continue reading.

> Damica bounces The Baby on her knee. Norma looks away from their conversation out the window where automobiles are slowing and then starting under the sway of the stop sign.

"But this is my story," Norma tells Dirty Norma. "God," she says. "You think you own everything." The Normas continue reading.

> Dead Elm Street was named for a blight that struck in 1937 and laid waste to fifteen trees that once lined Elm Street. Some of the trees weren't even sick yet, but the town had to cut them all down in order to stop the spread of the disease. And then they changed the name of the street.
>
> Damica's talking. "If it's all the same to you I'll—"
>
> "It's never all the same," Norma says, raising her voice this time.
>
> "I'll just get your lunch tomorrow. All I have is a twenty."
>
> Norma ignores her. She can't believe Damica is going to stick her with the bill again. She takes that day's paper from her purse, opens it up between them, and, bypassing the front page's headlines, flips to her favorite column, hiding in its pages.

HOUSE OF MUFFLERS DECLARES
BANKRUPTCY

Drake and Kanakas celebrate a victory

Linda Kanakas, lawyer for Drake Industries, stated that justice had been served
as she and her client left the courtroom
yesterday. Judge Burger ruled that Marguerite Eddell, proprietor of House of Mufflers, was in trademark violation not only
for her unlicensed use of the word "of" in
advertising materials but also for the silent,
yet understood "the," as in "The House of
Mufflers." Eddell was fined twelve thousand dollars, a sum that Eddell complained
she "just couldn't pay." The Third United
City Bank will be handling her bankruptcy
claims.

Norma stops reading. There is a photo printed
beside the article. It is a picture of Linda Kanakas
at some sort of black-tie affair. She is wearing an
elegant black evening gown with the tiniest crystal
teardrops stitched into the bodice. There is a man
standing beside her, a man who has been cropped
from the photo except for one hand that is resting
on Linda Kanakas's arm. Norma looks very closely
at this hand. The blood rises in her neck.

"I have a story for them," Norma tells Damica,
hitting the paper. "Hector Donoso."

"Who?"

"Remember Mary Donoso and how her father got deported back to Honduras and she got bumped out of our school district because her family had to move into Section 8 housing because her mother couldn't afford rent anymore without Hector's paychecks?"

"Sort of," Damica says, petting The Baby's head.

"Linda Kanakas was the one who called INS on Hector."

"Hmm." Damica looks out the window. "Linda Kanakas," she says, and chews her lip. "That was a long time ago. Yeah, I remember." Damica looks Norma straight in the eye, as if trying to tell her something without saying it, as if she is Superman with X-ray vision. Damica exhales loudly. "Norm, how's it going?"

"What do you mean?"

"You know."

Norma knows what she means. "I got my period yesterday."

"Oh, honey. I'm sorry."

"Yeah."

"Listen, Norm, I have a friend who tried to have a baby for four years. Four years. Can you imagine?"

Yes, Norma thinks. *Yes, I can imagine that.*

"Well, what do you think happened?" Damica asks.

"I think that after four years she finally had a baby or else you wouldn't be telling me this story."

"Well, you're right. That's exactly what happened."

"How old was she?"

Damica looks cross and doesn't answer that question, so Norma knows that the girl was probably twenty-two years old or some other annoying age a lot younger than Norma. Or at least her husband loved her. "You know what did the trick?" Damica asks.

"What?"

"Adoption papers. I swear. You and Ted should fill out adoption papers, and then I promise you, you'll get pregnant."

"I'll think about it." But what Norma really thinks is that all the people who had babies after trying for fifteen minutes should just keep their mouths shut because they don't know shit about how this feels.

"I have to get going," Damica says. "Will you hold The Baby for a second while I get my stuff together?" Damica reaches her foot underneath the table, feeling for her diaper bag. She holds The Baby out for Norma to take.

Norma looks over the edge of the paper. "Let me pee first." Norma folds the paper, grabs her pocketbook, and slides out of the booth.

The stalls of the ladies' room are made of cool aluminum. Norma rests her head against this coolness. She doesn't actually have to pee. She just has to stand inside the metal walls of the ladies' room for a minute alone.

GIVE ME A CALL. 1-800-FUCKIN'A.

Norma fingers the writing. She pulls her cell phone from the very bottom of her purse and dials 1-800-382-5462.

"Hello?"

"Hello, 1-800-DUBL-INC. Doubles Incorporated, providing goods and services for the Procreation by Division Industries. How may I help you?"

Norma swallows hard.

"Hi, yeah. Can I talk to someone in Customer Service?"

"Please hold one moment while I transfer your call."

Norma holds. The Muzak kicks on. "Sometimes when we touch, the honesty's too—"

"Hello. Doubles Incorporated. How can I help you today?"

Norma loves that song.

After lunch Norma takes a left off Dead Elm Street onto Larre Road, pronounced "Larry." Norma can't stand people who have cars that work. Everyone, it seems, drives a brand-new car. And all these new cars have perfectly functioning air conditioners. No one drives with the windows rolled down. There are no clunkers on the roads anymore, and to Norma this is a sign of America's great moral failure. Which is why about two months ago, about the same time her car broke down for good and she didn't have enough of her own money to replace it and Ted told her he wouldn't buy her a new one since she hadn't taken care of the first one he bought her, Norma began, slowly at first, dragging her house keys across the doors and hoods of other people's cars. She didn't think what she was doing was that bad in light of all the other things she could have done. For example, she could have started carrying a bowie knife to puncture tires or a screwdriver to pry open the hoods of other people's vehicles and unscrew their oil filters or slice the coolant hoses or reverse the positive and the negative cables on a car's battery. She hadn't done any of those horrible things. She hadn't started blowing up car dealerships yet. No.

Norma takes a right, turning up the driveway of the home for troubled people. She slips inside. "Hello?" she calls, but no one answers. Norma makes her way up a central staircase that twists smoothly as she goes. "Hello?" she calls again, but there is no answer. Norma goes right. "Hello?" she says. She glances behind herself and up overhead. She freezes. Directly above her the ceiling is horribly stained. A large brown mass of dripping discoloration that, because it has spread out in awkward and uneven rings, seems to throb. There must be a leak, Norma thinks, staring at the stain, studying its contours. She circles below it, without taking her eyes away from the mark, neck craned backward, arms linked across her chest. She stares, mesmerized. The stain looks a little bit like a fetus, a fetus with four legs.

"Boo."

And there she is.

Norma has a question for Dirty Norma. "Where'd you come from?"

"Where do you think I came from?"

"Well, I heard about this thing. Procre—"

"Procreation by Division for Morons?"

Norma says nothing.

Norma also says nothing.

"It's just, I'd been trying to have a baby for a long, long time."

"Oh boy. They really got your number. What'd it cost you? That thing's a racket. R-A-C-K-E-T! Plus," she says. "Those kits never work. Did you get it at Walmart? Their kits NEVER work."

"Then where'd you come from?"

"Guess," Dirty Norma says.

"This again?"

"Guess."

But Norma knows she's lying. Norma knows exactly where Norma came from.

She'd paid the extra $19.95 so that they would ship it express. "Sign." The deliveryman had thrust his handheld computer clipboard in front of Norma's face for her to sign. The box was no bigger than a supermarket paperback. *That can't be it*, Norma thought. But it was. She signed. He shoved the package forward. That was it. The deliveryman was gone and Norma was left holding her Home Procreation by Division kit. She waited in the doorway, staggered. She looked left, looked right. She disappeared back inside the house.

Norma took the box into the kitchen and used a steak knife to stab it open. There was nothing to it. Norma felt like an idiot. Inside the box was a paper foldout of poorly photocopied instructions and a palm-sized petri dish with a cover and a bright red bottom. That was it. $67.98. *Magic Rocks*, Norma thought. *Sea Monkeys. Garbage.* She stepped back from the box, and for a moment she felt like such a fool that she was tempted to throw the whole thing in the trash. But she stopped herself. She walked away and checked in with the chat room. Not much had changed there. Still a bunch of women who couldn't have babies. She turned away from the computer. She chewed at the side of her lip. *I'll just read the stupid instructions.* So she did.

Remove lid from petri dish, being very careful not to touch inside the dish. Spit into the petri dish. Make certain you wait at least an hour after eating, drinking, or brushing your teeth. First-morning spit is the most effective, but spit from any time of the day can be used as long as you wait an hour after eating, drinking, or brushing your teeth.

Norma looked at her watch. It was probably at least an hour. She collected a small pool of saliva in her mouth and, hanging her chin directly over the dish, she dropped warm spit from her mouth.

Cover the dish with the lid and set in a dry, sunny place to gestate.

Norma covered the dish, set it on a windowsill that gets afternoon sunlight, and turned back to the instructions to see what would happen next, but that was it. There were no more instructions. There was no *Soon you will notice*, or *Wait 24 hours*, or *If you encounter a problem, call*. There was nothing more.

The following morning Norma had forgotten about her science project. Fixing herself a pot of coffee, she saw the red dish. It wasn't where she'd left it on the sill. It was underneath their kitchen table. Someone had taken the top off and broken a bit of plastic off the side. Someone had ruined the whole damn thing. *It must be the cat*, Norma thought. *I mean, if I had a cat.*

Norma knows where Dirty Norma came from. She still has the package at home. The box is yellow and orange with a white starburst like a box of

Tide. She hadn't gotten it at Walmart. "You're not much like me."

"I'm exactly like you. Maybe you just don't like who you are." She rubs her back against the wall, an animal scratching. "Let's go look at the notebook. I'm worried about Mrs. Eddell."

Norma hadn't realized that Norma knew about Mrs. Eddell. "Whose notebook is that anyway?" Norma asks.

Dirty Norma turns once, flirting badly, a prostitute, paid to be there. She gives Norma a coy look. Norma follows her down the hall.

Norma was fired from her job at the Third United City Bank because she told a customer she'd be better off keeping her money at home in a coffee can hidden beneath her porch or bed, because sometimes the bank made "mistakes" and the mistakes were always in the bank's favor. She'd used air quotes. "Keep it at home," Norma whispered. "I do."

Norma's confidante was an older woman. That was why Norma had decided to reveal such a secret. She felt sorry for the older woman, wanted to help her. The woman turned out to somehow be related to the bank president, so Norma was let go, fired. She didn't make a scene as she had dreamed of doing. She didn't grab all the hundred-dollar bills from her drawer and spray them in a wild frenzy through the crowded lobby. Norma went quietly.

She'd behaved like a sane person. Where had that gotten her?

Recently unemployed, Norma's still adjusting to the new schedule. She takes midafternoon naps. She's sleepy all the time. Even now, here at the Institute with Dirty Norma. She lies back on the horribly stained bed, thinking, *Just a short nap*, but Dirty Norma won't have it.

"Come on. Let's read the notebook."

"You go ahead. I'm really sleepy all of a sudden."

"Maybe you're pregnant."

"I don't think so."

"No. Come on. We have to read it together." She tugs at Norma's arm, lifting her up into a seated position.

The suitcase is a small one, an older model, a hard-shell brown Samsonite with a leather edge, probably from the 1930s or 1940s. Just below the handle on the case is a simple golden latch and a monogram that is all but rubbed off. Thumbing the square of brass, Norma slides the catch to the left and pops the suitcase's lock. The inside is lined with forgotten pink taffeta.

She picks up the book and both Normas start to read from the stenographer's pad.

In a coffee shop off Dead Elm Street, Norma scrapes up the last bits of her tapioca pudding, certain that Damica won't try to stick Norma, unemployed Norma, with the bill for their lunch if she only eats dessert.

"If it's all the same to you I'll—"

"Haven't you noticed, Damica, that it's never all the same? It changes a little tiny bit each time!" Norma screeches.

The Baby sits up quickly and draws its eyes wide open, staring across the table at Norma, as if pixies had just whispered some surprising secret about her into The Baby's ear. The Baby stares and Norma stares back. "God, it's so creepy the way he just stares at me."

Damica says nothing.

Norma takes today's paper from her purse and opens it up to block out The Baby's stares. Bypassing the front page's headlines, Norma flips to page eleven, where her favorite column regularly appears.

EDDELL'S SAD END
Drake and Kanakas Back in Court
The body of Marguerite Eddell was found last night, the victim of an apparent suicide. A note with the body claimed she couldn't bear "new developments," perhaps referring to a backroom deal that allowed Mr. Drake to purchase the House of Mufflers from the Third United City Bank for a price considered far below market value. "It was

all I had left of my husband and now that it is gone, so am I," the note read.

Mr. Drake now owns six local businesses.

Kanakas and Drake found themselves back in court yesterday beginning proceedings against Tom Best Cadillacs for use of the word "best" in his advertising. Mr. Best claims, "It's not copyright infringement, it's my last name." To which Ms. Kanakas responded, "Too bad his parents didn't purchase the trademark."

"I have to go," Damica says. "Will you hold The Baby for a second?"

Norma looks over the edge of the paper. Norma folds the paper and slides out of their booth without saying anything.

The stalls of the ladies' room are made of cool aluminum. Norma dials frantically in the locked stall.

"Hello. You've reached 1-800-DUBL-INC. Doubles Incorporated, providing goods and services for the Procreation by Division Industries. How may I direct your call?"

"Customer service."

"One moment please."

"Hello. Customer service. How may I help you?"

"Umm. I think it happened."

"What's that, dear?"

"I bought your Procreation by Division for Morons and I, um, I think it happened."

"Mazel tov! Mazel tov!"

"Thank you?"

"You're welcome. Is there anything else I can help you with today?"

"Yes. I think something is wrong. I mean, I think something horrible is happening."

"What's that?"

"It seems like the world is splitting in two, or three. My husband is cheating on me."

"Yes?"

Norma fumbles a moment. "I thought procreation by division would be a good idea, but I changed my mind. Mrs. Eddell is dead, and with Mr. Drake owning everything, the more we get the less we have somehow. I mean, I wanted something, but then when I got it, it wasn't at all what I had wanted." She exhales, exasperated, into the receiver. "I mean, it's like when you eat too much of that kind of bread that expands like fog in your stomach?" Her voice is gaining speed. "I mean, how can there become more of something but it feels like it's less and less? I mean—" Norma takes a deep breath. "I mean—"

"You're not making any sense. Could be the Genomic Discordance."

"What's that?"

"It's kind of like what happens to pure-breds. You know, how their eyelashes start growing on the inside of their eyes or their hips get hobbled and then they can no longer walk. Thoroughbreds and corporate offices. Stuff like that."

"Is there any way to stop it?"

"Yes, but it's a bit complicated."

"Tell me!" Norma yells.

"Remember in the movie *Superman* when Christopher Reeve flies backward around the earth so quickly that he forces the rotation of the planet to move in the opposite direction, backward in time?"

"I remember," Norma says, then thinks, *Isn't Christopher Reeve dead?*

"That might work," the operator tells her.

"I'm scared," Norma says. "I never realized she'd have a mind of her own. She scares me," Norma says.

"Hmm."

"What? What hmm? What do you mean by hmm?"

"Well, it's just . . . Well, that's funny is all because, well, she said the same thing about you."

Just then the ladies' room door swings open. Norma quickly hangs up the phone. She flushes the empty toilet and opens the stall door.

It's Norma.

"Hello."

"Hi."

"I thought I'd save you the trip out Larre Road."

"But I like Larre Road. I like the quiet."

"It's just such a hassle, isn't it?"

"No."

"Boy, I thought you'd be grateful. I went through all this trouble to save you time."

"Umm, thanks. I guess."

"You're welcome."

"So what's going to happen now? The story is just going to get smaller and smaller until all that's left is a *U* or a *C* and even that starts to get cut up into nonsense, into tiny little unrecognizable bits?"

"It's more convenient that way. Efficient, you know."

"That's too bad. I really used to love walking out Larre Road. How I could stand where it changed from meadow to pine forest, where the air turned damp and the sidewalk got darker with that moss that grows in from the sides. Or how the sky would get blocked out by the pine boughs so none of my best thoughts could ever escape up into the atmosphere. Something like that."

"I have the stenographer's pad right here."

"Don't you want to just stop for a moment? Be slow?"

"No." Dirty Norma shakes her head.

Norma's cell phone starts to ring. She digs down into the bottom of her purse to pull the phone out. It's Ted. "One second," she tells Dirty Norma, answering her phone.

"Norma," Ted says. "Norma, we have to talk."

"I'm kind of busy."

"Norma, you have to help me. Norma, I, I don't have th—AHHG! I mean, I don't have words to, oh, Norma. I made a mistake. Norma, you're my wife. You are a part o—AHHG!—me."

"Ted. You're not making any sense."

"Oh, Norma!"

"Ted, is Linda there?"

"Linda?"

"Yes, Linda."

"Yes."

"Can I talk to her?"

"Oh, Norma," he says, and exhales loudly. "I wish I could tell you. You were th—AHHG!—bes—AHHG!" Like he's being electrocuted or something. He gives up. He passes the phone to Linda.

"What do you want?" comes a voice Norma hasn't heard since tenth grade.

There's got to be a way to stop it. It's

complicated, but Norma can handle complicated. "Meet me after school. By the jungle gym. Don't be late." Norma is trembling. She has never spoken to an upperclassman like that before. She hangs up the phone, and as she is returning it to her purse she feels a sharp stab. Something sharp in her purse. "Ow!" Norma says.

"What?" Dirty Norma asks.

"Nothing." But Norma knows exactly what pricked her. It's the bowie knife that she uses for puncturing tires. She slips her hand back into her purse and grabs hold of its handle.

"Here," Norma says, shoving the notebook in front of Norma. They sit down on a lowered toilet seat together. Both Normas start to read from the stenographer's pad.

In a coffee shop off Dead Elm Street Norma realizes once again that she is not pregnant. She hangs her head in her hands for a bit, crying alone in the stall. "Next month," she tells herself. "Maybe next month."

She turns left onto Larre Road. Pronounced "Larry." Larre Road reminds her of how she used to feel upon returning to class in junior high after lunch to find that the afternoon activity included a filmstrip viewing. Back when slow still existed.

"Psst. Come on! This way!" And into the tunnel she goes.

She returns to her homeroom. Her stomach is full of lunch. She is trembling. She has never spoken to an upperclassman like that before. After school she is supposed to meet Linda Kanakas. There is going to be a fight. Norma trembles. Norma touches the knife in her purse.

Norma's teacher, Miss Novak, says, "Take a seat, children. This afternoon we are going to watch a filmstrip."

Miss Leonard, the librarian, enters the classroom pushing a film projector on a wheeled cart that rattles across the linoleum floor. Miss Leonard tells Miss Novak, "Please be kind. Please rewind."

"All right, children. Let's have a seat." Miss Novak smiles, and as Norma sits down, Miss Novak shuts out the lights and pulls the blinds. The room is dark. Miss Novak presses play on the tape recorder. The first DING signals her to advance the filmstrip. "The Wonderful World of Mammals."

"See the gorillas at play," says the tape-recorded voice. Norma already feels drowsy. She settles into her daydreams, visions of the world to come, a future bright and gleaming she's read so much about, a marriage, someday children. "Gorillas, just like humans, have hair." DING. "Gorillas nurse their young just like humans."

The room is warm and dark. Norma's so drowsy. Time can move so slowly when packaged into the squares of an afternoon filmstrip. Time can even go backward in a filmstrip. The radiator hisses with its steam heat. Norma is so sleepy.

DING. "When challenged, gorillas will defend their territory. Gorillas will attack." Through closing lids Norma sees two gorillas fighting. One gorilla runs up a banana tree to escape. The other gorilla rips the banana tree from its roots, kills the other gorilla, kills the banana tree.

DING. "The strongest gorilla becomes the leader of the pack and gets to choose his mates. He chooses the most attractive mates." DING.

The filmstrip shows two gorillas named Ted and Linda mating.

Norma's head falls off to one side. DING.

"Don't let her get away!" Linda yells to her posse of sub-bullies. They are dressed just like Linda, a gang of lawyers in navy-blue suits, brown leather shoes. Norma gives chase. She leads the gang away from the jungle gym, out of the school, and down Dead Elm Street. Or at least it looks like Dead Elm Street. Towns can look so similar these days.

Norma takes a right onto Larre Road. The swarm of bullies follows, frothing like a pack of wild dogs. No time to go slowly. They are a mob, an anonymous mob. Norma barely recognizes them. Norma is beginning to sweat. Norma surges ahead.

"Get her!" Linda yells.

They pass through the place on Larre Road where the forest grows thick. Norma is running so fast that the grove of trees appears as only a blur. She takes a right up the driveway of the home for troubled people.

"Faster!" Linda is screaming, and the pack of wild girls renew their purpose at the sound of their leader's voice. They are gaining on Norma.

She takes the stone steps in one flying bound and grasps the door latch. It is locked. The Institute closed only a few months earlier.

"Psst! C'mon! This way! Quickly!" It is Dirty Norma. She's standing off to the left, at the corner of the Institute. She is looking down behind the building, into the backyard, as if she were standing at the entrance to some secret tunnel. She is pointing Norma toward the pool. Norma takes off running in that direction. She flies down the stone staircase and down the side of the building, rounding the corner where Dirty Norma is standing; she can feel the hot breath of the bullies behind her. Norma heads straight for the swimming pool, circling her legs so fast they resemble the propeller of a small airplane. At the very edge of the pool Norma launches herself across the gaping concrete hole. She is suspended in time for just a moment. Norma stretches even farther, growing taller as she does. With one arm she catches the far edge of the pool. She pulls herself up to solid ground and turns to watch the pack of cruel girls approach. They will surely all break their necks. They will tumble into the empty concrete pool. They will puncture holes in their lungs or jugulars and die. They will scream for dear life, falling like buffaloes off the cliff edge, down into the abyss below.

Norma dusts herself off. She turns around quickly. She can't let that happen.

"Stop! Wait! Linda! Stop! Linda! Look out! There's a pool! STOP!"

There is a way to stop this.

But Linda Kanakas, blind with anger,

rushes at the hole and throws herself across it, screaming, a war cry. The mob of lawyers/girls stops quickly behind her, halting their run just before the pool. They watch Linda fly across the abyss. They watch as Linda, with one arm, grabs the edge. Norma hears Linda's body crash into the side below. She can see Linda's hand grabbing at the side, holding on, trying to dig her fingers into the concrete and dirt. The hand writhes with all the life it holds. Norma's knife dangles by her side. With one deft hack, Norma could easily cut the hand from off its person and Linda Kanakas's body would crash down into the bottomless pit of Grady's old swimming pool.

Norma drops the knife. There's a way to stop this. Norma grabs hold of the hand and pulls Linda Kanakas to safety.

Both girls lie back, panting for breath.

The mob of girls, disappointed by the lack of violence and bloodshed, disperses.

"Why didn't you kill her?" It's Dirty Norma. She's standing above Norma, looking down. "She was going to kill you," Dirty Norma says.

"I know. It's just, I'm tired. This has gone on too long. I'm really, really tired," Norma says.

"Maybe you're pregnant."

Norma doesn't even bother to answer this time. Linda lies still. Norma thinks she can hear her silently sobbing. Norma has a seat beside Norma.

"Let's finish up, then. There's only a few pages left and I really want to know whether or not you kill Linda, because there's always the chance that at the last minute she might just spring to action. She might grab your knife and plunge it into your heart, or maybe she'll just strangle you. Maybe she'll just sleep with your husband, give you chlamydia, and ruin your chances for ever having your own babies."

"I don't think so. I don't think so," Norma says. "If I kill Linda Kanakas once, I'll just have to keep on killing Linda Kanakas over and over and over again into infinity. I don't want to do that. I'm too tired."

Dirty Norma says nothing. She looks annoyed by such a simple answer. She looks like she's got something else in mind. She draws the stenographer's pad from her back pocket.

The Normas lean against each other. Dangling their legs over the edge of the pool, the pool that could have been filled with dead girls but, because of Norma, isn't. They are both about to start reading from the stenographer's pad when Norma grabs the notebook from Dirty Norma's hand and dangles it over the hole. "Let's not do this," she says. "I don't want to know how it ends."

"You don't? But we've come so far. It seems like we have to go through with it."

"Can't you already kind of guess what's going to happen?"

"No."

"Well, I can."

"Then go ahead, guess."

"Well. Either good will win—"

"Or else bad will."

"Yeah, but which one is it?"

"Good or bad?"

"I can't quite tell yet."

"Well, guess," Norma says. "Guess."

ACKNOWLEDGMENTS

Thank you to the MacDowell Colony, the Peter S. Reed Foundation, Pratt Institute, and Bard College. Thank you, Jeannette Haien Ballard. Thank you, PJ Mark, Jenna Johnson, and Joe Hagan. I also gratefully acknowledge the magazines and anthologies where these stories were originally published:

Tin House: "All Hands" and "Beast"
The New Yorker: "The Yellow" and "Cortés the
    Killer" (as "Three Days")
FiveChapters: "The House Began to Pitch"
This Is Not Chick Lit: "Love Machine"
H.O.W. and *The Sunday Times*: "Wampum"